THE THRESHING FLOOR

Book 2 of The Elijah Chronicles

By
Ray Bentley
and
Bodie Thoene

Research by Brock Thoene

©

2019

Cataloging-in-publication data on file with the Library of Congress

Cover Design by Tyler Novak and Zach Andrews for raybentley.com
Interior Design by NewTypePublishing.com

Produced by www.raybentley.com
ISBN: 978-1-949709-62-9

Printed in the United States

Dedicated to Dorothy Jean Bentley

We are confident, yes, well pleased rather to be absent from the body and to be present with the Lord.

II Corinthians 5:8

PROLOGUE
November 10, 1938

Dead Jews littered the cobbled lanes of Nuremberg's Jewish Quarter.

Sides of buildings desecrated by graffiti: *Tod für Juden.*
DEATH TO JEWS

Electricity to the Sephardic Synagogue cut off.

And the Nazi Brown Shirts were still coming.

Candles illuminated the prayer books of two hundred swaying Jews who prayed the final, desperate prayers for deliverance from the book of Daniel.

"O Hashem, as befits Your abundant benevolence, let Your wrathful fury turn back from Your city Yerushalayim, Your Holy Mountain; for because of our sins and the iniquities of our fathers,

Yerushalayim and Your people have become a mockery among all who are around us."

Moonlight and the ominous glow of burning Jewish buildings shone through the four-hundred-year-old stained glass windows. Above the heads of the doomed congregation were scenes depicting the seven days of creation, the fall of man, and the great flood that had lifted up Noah's Ark. Color and light wordlessly told the stories portrayed in the Torah.

Seventeen-year-old David ben Elijah, son and heir of the Chief Rabbi, craned his neck upwards to ponder the image of Father Abraham offering his only son, Isaac, to God. The ram God had provided for sacrifice struggled in the thicket.

David knew well that Abraham's faith was so great he would have sacrificed his only son in obedience to the command of the Lord. And yet the ordeal had only been a trial to test Abraham's great faith.

He wondered as the sounds of shattering windows and the roaring of Hitler Youth and Storm Troopers drew near, was this terrible night of destruction and persecution also meant to test the faith of the Jews of Germany?

"Save us, O Lord!"

Until this night, David could not have imagined anything more fierce than the wrath of God. But this was Nuremberg, the terrible gathering place of tens of thousands of Nazis. They congregated here with burning torches to proclaim their adoration of their Fuhrer! There was no field large enough to hold all the marching hordes who came to hear the speeches of the party leaders. This was the city where the laws against the Jews had first been passed.

Now Hitler had taken note of the Great Synagogue and the Jewish Quarter of the city. He had studied the city map and the Jewish boundary. With a sweep of his hand, he had condemned the ancient Jewish section to destruction. Because Hitler willed the extinction of all Jews in Germany, the Great Synagogue of Nuremberg was to be destroyed tonight.

"Save us, Lord! We call upon you, O Adonai! For the sake of your Name!"

David watched his father lead the prayers of the congregants. "Again, we are destined to wander in the wilderness." Tears streamed down his father's lined cheeks. "Unless we have a miracle."

"Ascribe unto the Eternal, glory and might!"

David's father went to the Ark where the Holy Torah scrolls were kept and opened the doors for the last time. Reverently the Word of God was removed, unwrapped from its covering, cradled like a baby, kissed, and passed from man to man.

The groaning tracks of the demolition equipment could be heard outside. From the gallery, a university student snapped photographs of the mob hurtling down the lane.

David gathered the scroll into his arms. It was said this scroll was over seven hundred years old. The pain of David's grief nearly dropped him to his knees. "*Ascribe unto the Eternal, the honor due unto His Name.*" He kissed the scroll and passed it on.

"The voice of the Lord resounds above the waters!"

Outside the synagogue, a bulldozer, a tank, and a crane with a wrecking ball rumbled into place.

"Tear it down! Tear it down!"

"Not one stone left upon another!"

"Juden swine! Out! Out!"

Inside the synagogue, David's father shouted over the din. "The voice of the Eternal thunders above the mighty waters. The voice of the Eternal in strength."

"Destroy the Jews! Bring it down on their heads! Down with their Temple!"

"The voice of the Eternal doth shatter the cedars of Lebanon!"

A bullet smashed through a stained-glass window. The colorful scene burst into a thousand shards. Gleaming shrapnel rained down on the heads of the men in their silk prayer shawls.

Gleeful voices shouted, "Blow them up! Kill them all! Burn them!"

David's father touched his arm. Faded blue eyes searched the face of the young man. "It's time. You are my only son, David. The last. You know what you must do."

"I won't leave you, Father," David cried.

"You must go!" The old man commanded calmly. "It is arranged."

Others turned to gaze upon the parting of father and son.

The young man with a camera descended from the gallery and slipped a roll of film into David's pocket. "I got them all. Hitler's friend, the Grand Mufti of Jerusalem, is down there right in the middle of *SS* officers. I got all their faces on film. Take care of this, David. Deliver it to the BBC. One day the world will see what they have done. Our Testimony."

The President of the Congregation spoke, "David, you are the last. We are counting on you to survive."

"How can I leave you?"

David looked up at the window of Abraham raising his knife to slay Isaac. This was true faith, yet David's father would not permit David to stay and fight and die for the sake of the Name.

"My son. My only son. You must live," the Rabbi said. "You will be our witness."

"Papa!" David's tears overflowed.

The old Rabbi stooped to pick up a palm-sized fragment of glass from the ruined window, studied it a moment, and wrapped it in a kerchief. He passed it to his son. "Keep this and know, as long as there shall be a remnant, like this piece of glass, Israel lives. My son, remember who you are, and where you come from! You must live! The way of escape is provided. We prepared for this moment. Turn your face to Yerushalayim. For the sake of your people, Israel. For the sake of the covenant! Don't look back!"

What was the image on the shard?

David embraced his father in a final farewell, and then passed through ranks of hands reaching out to touch him in blessing as he left them. "Remember us . . . remember us . . . remember us . . . "

Descending to the dark synagogue basement, David made his way through a long tunnel, emerging into a tailor's shop two blocks away. It had all been arranged.

Quickly he changed from his clothes into a finely tailored German suit with the British passport and travel papers and money sewn into the lining.

"Don't look back," he admonished himself as he arrived on the street.

Gunshots erupted; the shouts of the attackers and the cries of the dying echoed around him. A Jewish grocer was pulled from his house and executed as the man's wife and children were forced to watch.

The boom and crash of the wrecking ball against the synagogue cupola resounded as David carefully made his way toward the safe house.

PART I

1

SPRING, 2018

5:12 a.m. Hadassah Hospital Trauma Unit, Jerusalem, Israel

Jack Garrison dozed fitfully beside Bette Deekmann's ICU bed. He was dimly aware of the unrelenting hums and beeps of monitors and the breathing rhythm of the ventilator keeping Bette alive.

For a moment, Jack could not remember where he was. The sounds of medical machinery clamped him to the memory of a London hospital the night his wife, Debbie, clung to life after a head-on collision.

Debbie and their baby had not survived.

And now?

Jack forced himself to open his eyes; forced himself to return to the present. This was a new nightmare. He was in Jerusalem, not England. This was the best-equipped trauma ward in Israel, which meant it was among the best in the world.

But the pale, young woman in the ICU bed was Bette. His beautiful, vibrant Bette.

Tubes everywhere. Wires everywhere. Fluids dripping in and out. The odor of bleach mixed with sickness; sweat produced by fear and anxiety.

His head throbbed with the present reality. A sense of dread and impending loss; the hope and hopelessness of waiting for a breakthrough . . . every emotion felt too familiar.

Jack shifted in the reclining chair, trying to find a more comfortable position. Through the glass partition, he spotted the surgeon who had operated on Bette. No longer in his scrubs, the doctor leaned against the nurses' station and spoke quietly to the Charge Nurse as he studied a chart. Both glanced up at the same moment and looked grimly toward Bette's room.

Okay, Jack thought, trying to interpret their expressions. *So it isn't looking so good.*

Jack needed answers. He ran a hand over his unshaven cheek and stood. How could anyone reconcile the ironies of this fragile life? There had been three surgeries piecing Bette Deekmann's intestines back together after the terrorist attack that had almost taken her life.

But, infection had flared yet again.

The doctor had explained to Jack: "This was a severe stomach wound. She's lucky to be alive. It is very, very difficult to get under control."

So surgery number four was scheduled. Jack prayed this would be the last.

The monstrous equipment contrasted dully with Bette's perfect feet; pink nail polish and still-cheerful painted daisy on her big toes.

Lingering at her bedside a moment, he tenderly touched Bette's swollen hand, then went out to speak with the surgeon.

"Good morning, Jack." The surgeon spoke in heavily accented English. Dark eyes betrayed the seriousness of Bette's condition and invited Jack to voice his questions.

"Yes, it's morning, isn't it?" Jack replied. His gaze lingered on the chart written in Hebrew.

"One can lose track of time in here. You should take a break."

"Can you tell me . . . still critical?

"Very critical. But . . . she is with us still, yes? A fighter. Truly. Anyone else, perhaps not. But she is physically strong and has such a will to live."

Jack nodded. "Yes. Yes. But . . . is there any improve-ment? And when will we know?"

The physician sighed and chose his words carefully. "This will be a long, slow process. Perhaps a few days. She is heavily sedated; unaware that you are here. I suggest you go home and sleep."

"Has anyone called her family? She told me her mother and father are in Singapore. But a large, extended family here in Israel, she said. A big family, she told me. But I'm the only one who has been by her bedside, except for her colleagues checking in."

The doctor glanced at the Charge Nurse. "Family?"

The stocky woman seemed surprised by the question. "I'm sorry, Mr. Garrison. There is no one to call."

Jack frowned. "She mentioned . . . Gal Gadot. A cousin."

The surgeon smiled. "Ah, yes. Wonder Woman. A little joke among us. We say all our Israeli Defense Force women are second cousins to Wonder Woman."

"But . . . her parents?" Jack stammered. "Brothers? In Singapore? They should be coming back to Israel. Do they even know what's happened?"

Physician and nurse exchanged an uneasy look. "Perhaps you should ask her superior officer?" the doctor suggested. "Yes. Perhaps. But for now, Jack, you should go home and get some sleep, yes?"

Jack rubbed his aching eyes and looked through the glass at the small, frail figure in the bed. "Thanks. But please: if there is any change . . . either way . . . you have my number. I'll be back this afternoon."

"Of course. You are on the contact list."

Jack reentered the dim cubicle and hovered above Bette for a long moment. Her lips curved around the clear ventilator tube. Jack whispered, "Please, God. Please let her live. Bring her back. This time, make it different." Then, "I love you, Bette." He carefully leaned through the tubes and wires of the hospital bed to kiss her goodbye.

What was it Bette had told him about never parting without saying, 'I love you?' Something about never knowing if this might be the last time in this life to see someone you loved.

Jack felt the truth of her warning. The monitor above her head charted a heartbeat, which kept her moored to life by a thin, jagged thread.

"I love you, Bette," he whispered again. One final, tender, touch of farewell.

An IDF sentry was at the door as Jack exited the critical care unit and made his way toward the family waiting room.

Lev, his face pained, stood up as Jack entered. "Hey, buddy." The two men embraced.

"The stomach wound," Jack explained. "Infection. They've got to open it up again; let it drain. She's in an induced coma. On a ventilator."

"Okay. Okay, Jack. Tough stuff. Come on, then. Let's get out of here awhile. What do you say?"

Jack followed him to the elevator. "I'm afraid to leave."

"I know. But your heart stays here. And we won't stop pounding on heaven's door until we get an answer."

The skies above Jerusalem were pale blue as the friends stepped outside. Jack inhaled deeply, breathing in fresh air and expunging the smell of hospital disinfectant. Windswept clouds blocked the sun. He asked, "What time is it?"

"Six o'clock. Have you had breakfast?" Lev took his arm and headed toward the car park.

"What day?"

"It's Wednesday. You're in bad shape."

"I can't stay away long."

"Sure. Let's get you back to your hotel. A shower and a nap . . . and some food, maybe."

"I'm telling you, Lev." Jack held back a sense of panic as they pulled to the entrance of his hotel. "I can't stay away too long."

"I get it. But this is all going to take some time, okay? Go on up. I'll come up as soon as I park."

Jack unfastened his seatbelt, but still hesitated. "Somebody needs to contact her family, Lev. I thought the IDF would do it. Bette told me about her family. She has a huge family. They need to know. Her parents are in Singapore, she said."

"This is all over the news. They've probably seen it."

"Then where are they?" Exhaustion suddenly overwhelmed him.

Lev took it in. "Man, you gotta rest. Look at you. I'll see what I can find out."

✧ ✧ ✧

Located in East Jerusalem where Rub'a el-Adawiya Street made a looping turn to the east, the Mount of Olives lunch counter possessed two advantages as far as Omar Barghouti was concerned. It was a half block from the bus stop by which he had arrived, and it was perched on a hill with excellent visibility in all directions.

Outside the cafe were Coca-Cola crates, a row of two-liter plastic water bottles, and a blue-painted freezer offering popsicles and single-serving cartons of Nestle's ice cream. The faded lettering on the sign over the door was written in English, Arabic, and Hebrew. "Rooftop restaurant," it proclaimed.

The location was perfect for a meeting that needed to appear completely innocent.

The one who had called for this meeting, Rafa Husseini, was late, but not because of the traffic. It was just past six-thirty in the morning, and the street was empty of both cars and pedestrians.

Omar was not bothered by her tardiness. He leaned against the ice cream freezer, smoking a cigarette as if he had nowhere to be and nothing to do.

A block away, a once champagne Mercedes, now a
sallow tan, nosed into a spot on the sidewalk between
an electrician's work truck and a roll-off trash dumpster.
Without lifting his head or showing any interest, Omar
noted the female figure that emerged from the car. Though
middle-aged, she was dressed in Levi's, a purple sweatshirt
with the hood up, and hiking boots. The woman walked
straight past Omar without speaking, bought a coke at the
counter, and then went up to the rooftop terrace.

Taking his time, looking up and down the street, Omar
finished his smoke, then ground out the butt under his heel.

The flat roof of the establishment allowed a rusting
metal awning to provide shade for three picnic tables and
six chairs, two of which were missing their backs; the
advertised Rooftop Restaurant.

But the view was something else again. High enough to
scan across the intervening valleys and ridgelines, Omar's
perch revealed the breadth of Old City Jerusalem and the
skyscrapers of the modern city beyond. *That is ours; should
all be ours*, Omar thought. *Thank you, Jews, for your efforts. Now
vanish from the earth! No? Then let me assist you.*

Omar sat at one table and Rafa at another, though no
one else was on the roof. They sat in silence, gazing out
toward the west.

Rafa finally spoke. "Why did you choose this location?"

Omar snorted. "You're the one who said 'No' to
a meeting in Gaza City, and 'No' again to meeting in

Ramallah. It made me think you have something in mind that you don't want either your Hamas chiefs or your Fatah bosses to know about."

Rafa looked angry that her motivation was so transparent, but she couldn't argue with the conclusion. "This American president . . . this Trump," she began. "He must be . . . "

"Stop," Omar insisted. "Don't talk crazy."

Mastering her thoughts, Rafa continued, "He is going to recognize Jerusalem as the Jews' capital. And then he's going to move the American Embassy there."

"So? What do you expect me to do about it?"

"There is still time to prevent it!" Rafa insisted. "Protests in Gaza and the West Bank, but also showing the world . . . especially America . . . that it is not wise to go against the will of the Palestinian people."

"Hamas receives electricity from the Jews. The Palestinian Authority sends their teenagers to private schools alongside Jews and Christians. They make big noises, but they don't really do anything!" Omar complained.

"Which is why I come to you," Rafa continued. "I consult for both Hamas and Fatah, but my heart is with Palestinian Jihad just like yours."

Omar's eyes narrowed. The tips of his finger and thumb brushed the hilt of the knife tucked in his waistband. "Who says?" he demanded.

"Doesn't matter," Rafa returned. "Do you want to hear

about the job or not?"

Omar shrugged. "Talk. It's what Palestinian leaders do best."

Rafa explained how a highly placed, wealthy man in Britain had worked very hard to build and maintain anti-Israeli sentiment in Europe, only to see part of his labor undone by Jack Garrison. "He is an American professor, but he lives here. Now he works for a Christian group trying to build better and closer relations between Israel and the United States."

Omar lit another cigarette and blew a spiral of blue smoke toward a hole in the dilapidated awning. "Again, So?"

"He is also the grandson of one of the Jewish heroes of the Great Disaster," Rafa said, referring to the 1948 Jewish War of Independence. "Garrison also has a girlfriend who is with *Yamam.*"

"The Jewish anti-terror group. Wonderful. Could you pick any harder targets?"

"Don't you see?" Rafa corrected. "That's what makes them perfect! Take them all out, and we convince the world that a Jerusalem still enslaved by Jews is not and never can be safe for them."

"Nice speech," Omar noted. "How much?"

"Ten thousand, American. Five when you agree and the rest when the job is done."

Omar was impressed but also suspicious. "I think

there's more to this job than you are telling me," he suggested. "I don't think either Hamas or Fatah knows about your plan or my payment. Nor do I think you can afford me by yourself. If you are willing to risk a bullet in the back of your head for embezzling, then there must be a personal reason."

Rafa gripped the table until her nails scored little lines in the chipped paint. "The American blinded my brother, and the Jewish *sharmuta* killed him. I want them both dead."

✿ ✿ ✿

The surgery was finished. Bette was aware of the medical staff gathered around her. The sounds of alarms beeped far away.

"Blood pressure dropping . . . "

"We're losing her!"

"Bring her up!"

"Heartbeat . . . "

Bette felt herself rise slowly from the bed. Suddenly, she was an observer as the world around her became covered in a gauzy veil. There were the doctors. The nurses. She saw them from above, all working frantically on a young woman laying ashen and unresponsive in a hospital bed.

Bette studied the patient, somewhat surprised there was another person sharing her room. Who was it? When did they bring her in?

A doctor shouted the name, "Bette! Bette! Come back to us, girl!"

Bette finally recognized herself. Her face. Her body. The medical staff was fighting desperately; commanding her to live. The man in charge worked to make her heart beat, and demanded that her spirit not leave.

Above it all, Bette smiled.

She felt the presence of someone beside her. Suddenly she was no longer in the hospital room but somewhere else; a beautiful place filled with light and music and a sense of peace so powerful that she no longer heard the sounds in the hospital room, or the people calling her to come back. She did not want to return to that place of pain and suffering.

Who was this man that appeared next to her? Not someone she knew, and yet he seemed familiar. An angel? Her angel?

He was clothed in light. His eyes were honey gold, and he studied her with a kind expression on his face.

Bright beams of light flowed from his hands and from his feet and from his forehead.

"Bette." He spoke, and it was an embrace; as if her mother had rocked her to sleep and then said her name as she carried her to bed.

"I'm here, Lord," she replied, though her lips did not move.

"I have been waiting for you."

"Who are you?"

"I AM the one you have spent your life searching for."

"I was lost. And now I have found you."

"You were not lost. I have been beside you, watching over you all along."

"Please. Do you hear the cry of my people?"

He lowered his head and searched her face tenderly. "I hear them. I love them. Who will go to them for me? Who will speak to them for me?"

"I will go. If you send me, I will go for you."

The holy one smiled. "Yes. I knew you would. You must lay aside your life and pick up mine."

"Give up everything?"

"For a time."

Bette felt herself accept his offer. "Who should I tell them has sent me? What is your name?"

"You will find what you seek at Notre Dame. My gift to you is in the image of suffering."

Bette reached up, longing to embrace him. "Please, Lord! When will I see you again?"

"Soon, my daughter. But remember I am always with you."

His features faded into light. Suddenly, Bette found herself enshrouded by physical pain. Human hands and human voices touched and called out to her and to one another in victory and relief.

"Okay! We've got her!"

"Her blood pressure is rising!"

"Heart beating on its own again!" "Bette! Bette, honey! Can you hear me?"

Bette nodded. Her eyes fluttered open, and then closed again.

"Okay! A close one."

Bringing Bette back to full consciousness was a process that took days even after the infection was finally declared under control. Heart rate and blood pressure remained steady. At last, she was able to breathe on her own. The ventilator was removed during the early morning hours.

Jack daubed her mouth with a cool, lemon-flavored wash. She licked her lips and sighed. That was the first sign she was coming back from the deep, medically induced sleep.

He was at her bedside at sunrise when, at last, she opened her eyes, saw his face, and attempted a smile through cracked lips.

"Bette, I'm here," he whispered.

She tried to speak, but only croaked as her mouth formed his name and the question, "How long?"

"Don't try to talk." He stroked her forehead.

"How . . . long?" She rasped.

"You've been out quite a while. Fighting hard. But you're back now. You're going to make it."

She shook her head in frustration. She did not want to know how long she had been in the hospital. "Home," she breathed.

"Ah." Jack finally tumbled to her meaning. "You want to know how long 'til you can go home?"

She nodded.

He resisted the urge to laugh. "When you're well enough. Then."

She closed her eyes in a frustrated frown. "Home."

"Sure." He tried to reassure her. "But just try not to fight it. I'll be here. They'll want to know you're awake. I'll go fetch your nurse now."

A curt nod of acceptance. Jack slipped out of the room and stepped to the nurse's station.

"Okay. Ms. Deekmann is awake. And, big surprise, she wants to go home. Now."

The nurse laughed and pushed the call number for Bette's doctor. "I knew it was a good thing she was sedated. You know how many times she tried to pull out the ventilator tube and the IVs? Not exactly a cooperative patient."

"Well, she's awake and wants to go home." Jack shrugged.

"Lots of luck to us all. That day will still be a while," she said over her shoulder as she headed toward Bette's room. "Go get some breakfast. We'll ring if we need you."

✡ ✡ ✡

Jack raised his face to the hot water streaming from the hotel shower. Relief poured over him. "Thank you, God," he breathed. "Thank you for giving Bette back to me."

Even as he prayed in gratitude, he wondered, *What if she had died? Would I still believe in God if Bette hadn't made it?*

The answer was imponderable. Jack had lost his conviction when his wife and child died. But now, in Israel, everything seemed different. He had not returned to faith, but rather, trust in the love and grace of Sovereign God was born anew in him.

But doubt remained. Could he have gone forward, once again, with inconsolable loss? Was his love strong enough that he could let Bette go? Jack stepped out of the shower and put on the King David Hotel bathrobe. He was too tired, he thought, to try to measure the strength of his faith. Not now.

He fell into bed. No more introspection. All he wanted was a few hours of untroubled sleep and then to wake up in a world where everything was put right and there was no more doubt about anything. No more tears. No more sickness. Love with a good woman. Kids. Peace. A perfect world. A perfect life.

Not possible, but even so it was a nice image to go to sleep to.

"We're all still Adam, homesick for Eden," he said aloud to himself and smiled as he drifted off.

✧ ✧ ✧

Bette was aware of someone sitting beside her hospital bed. "Jack," she whispered, opening her eyes.

"No. Not Jack." The craggy face of her IDF Commanding Officer frowned back at her with an uncharacteristic expression of sympathy. "Me. Mordechai."

"Modi? What are you doing here?"

"What? I can't visit our best agent in the hospital?"

"Am I dying?"

"Almost died, I hear. But not quite." He smiled. "I would have been sorry to lose you."

"Yes. I'm sure of it. I almost flew away. Now I feel . . . not so good. Sick."

"You are a very strong girl to have survived all this." He shrugged. "The doctors tell me it will be a while until you're back."

Her throat still hurt from the ventilator. "I'm thirsty."

He reached for a glass on her bed tray. "Ice chips

only. They told me to give them to you if you asked." He spooned ice onto her parched tongue.

Relief. "Modi, you wouldn't come to visit unless there was a reason."

The furrows on Modi's forehead merged with a scar over one eye. "Okay. To the point. We have intercepted a conversation between the Hamas leadership. Bette, you were mentioned."

"You mean, the attack?"

"Yes. The attack, but I'm talking about you. Your family connection. Your possible identity."

Bette let the ice melt on her tongue. "So they know?"

"They expressed a suspicion only. But they mentioned your grandfather. Your father. The massacre."

Bette drew a deep breath. "What does this mean?"

"It was a brief reference. You know, 'the woman IDF soldier who killed our assassin is possibly related to . . . '"

"How could they know?"

"We don't have any more information. It's probably nothing, but we wanted you to be aware of it."

"What now?"

"We are keeping a bodyguard posted outside at your door for now. Not that anyone could get onto this floor, or into your room, but we want you to know there's still an extra layer of protection in place."

"Thank you. Thanks. And my brother?"

"No. Nothing at all about him. Not ever. Invisible. No

suspicion."

She closed her eyes in relief. "What about Jack?"

"You'll have to decide what to do about him, Bette. I warned you not to fall in love."

"Yes, you did. Thank you very much."

"So. I guess that's all." He patted her hand, careful not to touch the IV. "We have decided to transfer you to Tel Aviv for recovery if that helps. A little distance. Sea air. A little time to heal and think things through."

Bette nodded. Her eyes brimmed with tears. "Sure. Whatever you say, Modi."

✧ ✧ ✧

In the gathering twilight, streetlights popped on, beginning first in the depths of the Kidron Valley beneath the perch where Jack prayed on the Mount of Olives. The line of lamps climbed the slopes as daylight retreated, like torches carried by invisible hands. In the growing dusk, it was easy to imagine the electric globes were actually torches flaring and smoking against the cobalt Judean sky.

With growing conviction, he was, in fact, witnessing blazing firebrands. Jack was not surprised to find the robed figure of Eliyahu standing beside him. "So," he asked without fear. "Where are we this time? Or should I say, 'when?'"

Twenty-first century Jerusalem had disappeared: no

autos, no paved streets. So had eleventh century Jerusalem, the seventh, and the first. No longer were there any Christian Crusader buildings, or Muslim Domes or Roman fortresses . . . or even a Jewish Temple.

The flat expanse of rocky plateau Jack knew as the Temple Mount was bare. Extending from it toward the south on the point of a rocky outcropping was a primitive fortress roughly the shape of a spearhead. The land around the tip of the blade fell away sharply; sheer cliffs defined by the sides and intersection of two deep canyons. Vertical rock faces were surmounted by battlements of stacked stone. Low places and gullies had been filled with rubble to prevent anyone from using them to ascend the heights.

As if Eliyahu knew Jack had fully taken in the setting and was now ready for his question to be answered, the night was suddenly populated.

Mocking laughter echoed from the hilltop: "You will never take Jebus!" a hoarse voice jeered.

"Go back to your kingdom of Israelites . . . and your other sheep," another unseen figure scoffed. "Do you see these cliffs and these walls? A lone blind man and a single cripple could defend them . . . and one of them could go home to supper!"

Gales of sarcasm tumbled over the walls, rebounded from valleys, and deluged the canyons.

Torchlight illuminated the grim faces of warriors

standing on the hillside near Jack and Eliyahu. Bearded men in conical helmets wore leather vests and carried short swords and spears. Their robes were hitched up and belted to leave their legs bare at mid-thigh above sandaled feet.

The tallest of them, a ruddy-complected man whose hair glinted dark red in the firelight gestured with his sword toward the mockers on the heights. "I have been king in Hebron these seven years," the unmistakable chief of the group said. "Shall I return there with the laughter of the Jebusites ringing in my ears?"

"King David," Eliyahu murmured to Jack.

The soldiers of the Jewish king replied with growls and angry words. "Never!"

"The Almighty gave this land to your fathers and our fathers; to Father Abraham, and then the tribes," asserted one. "The rest of Canaan acknowledges you as king . . . and so will this place."

"Brave words," King David replied drily. "I have sworn that whoever strikes the first blow against the Jebusites will be the captain of my host. Will it be any of you?"

A clamor of voices responded. Some proposed a direct assault up the steep cliffs. Others suggested attacking the wall that defended the city at the edge of the tabletop plateau on the north. Others, more cautious, offered a siege. "We'll starve them out," one said.

A muscular figure with a hawk's beak for a nose and fierce eyes stepped forward along with two others of similar build and features. "I will strike the first blow," the volunteer swore, holding his sword hilt over his heart.

"So, Joab," David said. "And how many of my men do you need to make good on your promise? A hundred? Two hundred?"

Joab jerked his head left and right to the pair of warriors flanking him. "Just my brothers and I. So long as you surround the city on all sides. Just before moonset let the archers attack from the valleys and the sling-men from along the wall to the north. Let them be as loud as possible . . . think of Gideon attacking the Midianite camp. Keep a hundred swordsmen in reserve near the northern wall for when I open the gate.

"Only," Joab added, "let no torches appear, or any of our troops be seen just there." Joab pointed toward a clump of trees halfway up the pillars of jagged limestone.

Before any time had passed Jack and Eliyahu were threading their way into a cleft in the rock; the fourth and fifth members of Joab's raiding party, though unseen and unheard by the others. A fold in the rockface . . . hidden from view and protected from entry by a thorny grove of acacia shrubs . . . led to a hole just barely large enough for an armed man to wriggle through.

Once inside, Joab struck a flint rock against the edge of a dagger. The shower of sparks ignited a tar-covered torch with which he led the way forward.

"How did anyone find this place?" Jack wondered to

Eliyahu as he dropped to his feet in the shoulder-high passage behind the entry.

"This is the location of the thicket where the Almighty caused the ram to be caught by his horns. You remember: when Abraham brought his son Isaac to this mountain in obedience to the Lord's command."

Jack nodded. In another vision, he had witnessed the moment when Abraham's knife flashed in the sun over his boy's chest . . . and God had halted the Patriarch and then rewarded him and all his descendants for his committed faith.

Eliyahu continued, "Where the Almighty promised to bring Himself as the ultimate sacrifice. It was from the offspring of those acacia barbs that a crown of thorns was woven for the Messiah; the Son of David. Remember, everything means something!"

Abraham and Isaac . . . a substitute sacrifice . . . the King of the Jews tortured and mocked. Jack had much to ponder as the water-worn passageway snaked and curved and sloped downward inside the hill. The quintet passed some time in silence broken only by the sounds of their breathing and the slap of their sandals underfoot.

Jack heard the burble of water at the same moment Joab raised his fist to halt the movement. "We are near the bottom," the captain hissed. "From here on, we must make no noise at all and show no light."

Involuntarily, Jack pivoted toward Eliyahu and made a

shushing motion, forgetting for a moment they were only observers and not participants.

Joab's brothers nodded tersely as their commander snuffed out the torch, plunging them into utter blackness. Moments passed, and then the tiniest trickle of light cracked the dam of darkness. A faint glow gleamed high overhead as the cavern opened upwards. Shuffling forward, the raiders advanced until Joab suddenly tottered above an unseen precipice. His toe dislodged a pebble which fell into a hidden pool of water with a splash. Everyone froze, listening for the shouts of alarm that would signal they had been discovered.

No such call of warning came. Instead, the clash and cries of a distant battle, and more Jebusite taunts reached Jack's ears.

"Now we move and move quickly!" Joab ordered his brothers.

A waterskin, suspended from a knotted, camel-hair rope, hung in the middle of the cavern. Hand-over-hand, Joab and his kin ascended into the heart of Jebus.

Glancing back at Eliyahu, Jack objected, "I don't think . . . " before he saw Eliyahu's answering grin.

In the next moment, Jack was above ground, just inside the northern gate. Almost all the defenders were atop the walls surrounding the city. The unexpected attack inside the fortress caught the Jebusites entirely unawares. A trail of moaning wounded or silent bodies traced the path of Joab's assault. With his two brothers slashing on either side, Joab hacked the cords suspending the crossbeam that barred the gate . . . and the entry to Jebus was open.

A hundred warriors followed David's charge into the city.

Moments later, Jack watched a figure kneel at David's feet. "So, Araunah," David queried. "Is it to be peace or war? Life or death?"

"Let it be peace and life," the vanquished king agreed, plucking a circlet of gold from his head and pitching it onto the ground.

"And will you yield yourself in faithful service to me, and to my God?" David insisted.

"I will."

Lifting his voice so the whole mountaintop could hear, David shouted, "Then know this: from now on, this is my capital. The City of David, and of the God of Abraham, Isaac, and Jacob. From here I will rule over the city of peace Jerusalem . . . and my kingdom of Israel."

✧ ✧ ✧

It was almost eight o'clock in the morning when Jack emerged from the elevator into the lobby of the King David Hotel. Pilgrims were coming and going; meeting tour guides, and boarding vans and coaches for their holy adventures.

Dodi was already seated in the dining room when Jack arrived. In honor of moving the American Embassy to Jerusalem, she was elegantly dressed in royal blue with a white shawl, reflecting the colors of the Israeli flag.

He brushed her forehead with his lips and sat opposite her.

"You are very handsome today." Dodi plucked at the sleeve of his navy blue sport coat. She lowered her chin. "I don't believe I have ever seen you wear a necktie, much less a red tie. Very American."

"It seems to fit the occasion. Red tie, white shirt, and a blue suit. In honor of the American Embassy opening in Jerusalem. "

"A miracle, Jack. Prophetic. You know this. A true miracle."

Jack nodded. "I believe we will see the Messiah arrive soon."

"We all agree. So say the rabbis. So say the Christians. And meanwhile, as the prophets have written, all the world will go on eating and drinking and giving in marriage, until the hour overtakes them."

Jack gave his order to the waiter. "Right. Meanwhile, I'll have a full English breakfast."

Dodi studied the menu. "Oatmeal. Hot tea with lemon." The old woman leaned forward. Her bright blue eyes flashed. "And the giving-in-marriage part of the prophecy? Do I hear wedding bells ringing?"

Jack frowned. "Not yet. I'm reliving . . . so many memories."

From the kitchen came the sound of shattering glass as someone dropped a serving tray.

Dodi inclined her head. "Do I hear the sound of a heart-shattering?"

He shrugged. "Not quite so dramatic as that but . . . I don't know. The timing isn't right."

"Well, then. Be patient. You'll know when you are both ready."

He smiled wryly. "But you know there isn't time. Not enough time, anyway."

"It won't matter if life as we know it is interrupted."

"If Messiah is coming and time is short, I want to live every minute. Not a moment to waste."

"Time does not exist in eternity. And if our holy midnight is to strike soon in Jerusalem, we will carry our love with us. You. Bette. All will be well, believe me."

✡ ✡ ✡

There were throngs of people around the King David Hotel. Though far from being the most modern or most luxurious accommodations in Jerusalem, many tourists . . . especially Americans . . . preferred the pink limestone bulk of the almost ninety-year-old hostelry. Located at the nexus of Old and New Jerusalem, its walls breathed history.

It was the morning of the historic move of the U.S. Embassy from Tel Aviv to Jerusalem. Outside the hotel, a line of limos stretched up the street, each waiting their turn to pick up dignitaries, businessmen, and religious leaders.

Sandwiched as it was between Abraham Lincoln Street and George Washington Street, today the King David Hotel seemed even more American than ever.

Omar was not on the King David Hotel property. He was on the sidewalk of the YMCA across the street. Dressed in a polo shirt and wearing khaki slacks, Omar clutched a pair of miniature Israeli and American flags. In his hip pocket was an Egyptian passport, but so far no one had bothered to check it.

Even so, this whole exercise was futile. Every other pedestrian on King David Street was an IDF soldier. Omar suspected that one of every three or four supposed tourists was a plain-clothed Israeli security guard.

When President Trump stayed at the King David, Omar had heard there were a thousand people in his entourage. The Presidential Suite was fireproof, bombproof, and assault proof. In an unguarded moment, a hotel employee quipped: "If the hotel explodes, that whole room would go straight up in the air and come down again intact. There might be some broken bones, but no one would die." He was immediately fired.

No one would die today either, Omar thought bitterly. *I*

told that idiot Rafa Husseini this was pointless. "What a powerful statement it would be," she said. Ridiculous! I leave suicide bombing to easily persuaded teenagers. In this crowd, I won't even see the American, Garrison, or the old Jewish woman, let alone get close to them.

When an Israeli soldier looked his way, Omar waved the pair of flags and smiled.

✿ ✿ ✿

Jack held onto Dodi's elbow as they filed through the metal detectors and past the line of armed guards. The space in front of America's Jerusalem consulate, about to be rechristened as its embassy, was packed with dignitaries, special guests, and honorees. "I'm still amazed," Jack remarked in his grandmother's ear.

"Of course," she said. "It's an amazing day."

No," he corrected. "I'm amazed that you and I are here, in person, to see this happen. I wanted it so much for you, but the number of tickets was so limited and in such demand, I just . . . "

Dodi patted his hand. "Don't give it another thought."

It was Jack who was there as Dodi's guest instead of the other way around. Jack had called her, with great regret, to apologize that he had not been able to arrange their attendance. Dodi accepted the report of his efforts with thanks, then said, "As a matter of fact, the Prime Minster's office called the day before yesterday, to reconfirm my attendance. They asked if they could send a limo, but I told them my grandson would be driving me."

In recognition of Dodi's tireless work for Israel, and to honor the memory of her husband Sol, on this, the seventieth anniversary of Israeli statehood, Bibi Netanyahu had made a particular point of assuring Dodi was invited.

"After all," Dodi continued. "If Sol and I . . . and a lot of other brave boys and girls . . . had not helped Israel survive its first weeks of statehood and a lot of conflicts since, there'd be no seventieth anniversary to celebrate, eh? And no U.S. Embassy here either."

Dodi and Jack were five rows from the stage. When the speakers for the day's ceremonies arrived, Jack found that he and his grandmother were just three rows behind Ivanka Trump's right shoulder, and directly behind Prime Minister Netanyahu. Dodi and Jack had a better view than many American and Israeli notables did. "Good spot," Dodi observed, "as long as those two sit down." Two rows in front of her stood the Chief Sephardic and Chief Ashkenazi Rabbis of Israel. Both men were extraordinarily tall, and both wore broad-brimmed black hats that blocked the view as the audience rose to applaud the entry of the Marine Color Guard and the trooping of the colors.

The ceremony was under an immense awning, installed for the purpose, which sheltered the grandstands and the stage erected directly in front of the U.S. Embassy. "Nice,"

Dodi commented as the U.S. national anthem concluded. "This canopy . . . like a *chuppah*. Just right for a wedding. America and Israel have been engaged for a long time, but today is the wedding ceremony proper."

U.S. Ambassador to Israel, David Friedman, was introduced. In his opening remarks, he reminded the audience that it had been seventy years ago since the first prime minister of Israel, David ben Gurion, had proclaimed the Jewish state.

"And Sol and I were there," Dodi murmured. "Well, Sol was. I was in prison."

It took a moment for Dodi's comment to register. Jack blinked and stared at his surprising grandmother, but there was no time for questions.

"America's Congress voted to move the U.S. Embassy to Jerusalem in 1995," Dodi murmured. Her eyes narrowed, and her whispered words were clipped with suppressed annoyance. "And look, it only took four presidents and twenty-three years to make it become a reality."

President Donald Trump offered his congratulations by recorded video message, pointing out that every sovereign nation on earth had the right to name its own capital city, and that all three branches of the Israeli government were located in Jerusalem.

Of all the speakers it was Prime Minister Netanyahu who received the most enthusiastic response from the crowd. He thanked President Trump for making the move of the embassy a reality, and he also thanked the many friends of Israel who had prayed for and worked for this day. "By recognizing history . . . you have made history," he said. "I was three years old, holding my brother's hand . . . he was six . . . when I grew up not far from this very place."

"Near the Green Line separating Jewish from Arab territory," Dodi whispered to Jack. "No-Man's-Land between East and West Jerusalem."

"My mother," Netanyahu continued, "said I could go so far but no further, because of the Arab snipers." He asked the audience to compare that time in the early 1950s to the present day when Jerusalem was once again entirely controlled by Israel. The move of the U.S. Embassy to the Holy City was evidence of that change.

Bibi recalled the chronology of the Jewish presence in Jerusalem, each name and event punctuated by an emphatic nod of Dodi's head. Abraham and his sacrifice. King David's capital city. King Solomon and the Temple. The rebuilt Temple after the Exile. The purified Temple in the days of the Maccabees. All those who gave their lives, down to the historic announcement in 1967 by the Jewish troops who proclaimed, "The Temple Mount is in our hands!"

"A great day for a great partnership," Netanyahu said. "Seventy years after President Truman committed America to be the first nation to recognize the new state of Israel." The prime minister then quoted the word of the Lord as recorded by the prophet Zechariah, and Dodi mouthed the words in unison with him: "I will return to Zion, and dwell in the midst of Jerusalem. Jerusalem shall be called the City of Truth, The Mountain of the Lord of Hosts, The Holy Mountain."

When the ceremony broke up, Dodi and Jack stood rooted in place. "A historic day!" Dodi exulted. "A glorious, miraculous day."

"By international law, this consecrated ground where the embassy stands is American soil," Jack said. "Here in the heart of Jerusalem, America and Israel are forever joined."

"Oh, Jack," Dodi laughed. "Don't you know that America has always been an ally of the Jewish people's longing for home, ever since its beginning? America's blessings are all rooted here. You heard the good rabbi and Psalm 122: *Pray for the peace of Jerusalem. They that love thee shall prosper.*"

✡ ✡ ✡

Unable to prevent the embassy move, Palestinian anger boiled over and continued unabated. Piles of automobile tires along the border were already blazing, throwing out thick clouds of black, acrid smoke. Carried by gentle breezes off the Mediterranean Sea, the roiling current of tarry vapor drifted toward the fence and the tense line of

Israeli soldiers on the opposite side.

"See?" Rafa Husseini urged her teenaged warriors. "The smoke disguises our movements and will also cause any tear gas to be blown back toward the despicable Jews!"

Executive Director of Rights for Palestine, and special advisor to both Hamas in Gaza and the Palestinian Authority in the West Bank, Rafa could appear reasoned and diplomatic . . . but not today. Today, while the Great Satan, America, celebrated its partnership with Israel, Rafa was committed to showing the world the passion of Palestinian resistance to illegal occupation and tyranny.

"Remember *Nakba*!" Rafa reminded her army of thirteen- and fourteen-year-olds. "Remember 1948's Day of Disaster, when the Jews forced thousands of your parents and grandparents out of their homes. Today . . . and tomorrow . . . and every day, as long as necessary, we remind the Jews and the world that we insist upon return! We will have our homeland back! We will clean this land of its occupiers and their stench."

Besides her deep-seated hatred of Israel, Rafa had personal reasons for rage: her brother, Faisal, had been blinded in one eye by the American, Jack Garrison, and then killed by a Jewish policewoman. Revenge loomed large in Rafa's thoughts. Today was just a small repayment amid her bigger plans.

Wearing checkered *keffiyahs* as headscarves or facemasks, the boys screeched and cheered Rafa's words.

Shaking wooden clubs and fist-sized stones, they implored her to let them attack the fence. "We will break through!"

"We will overrun them!"

"Death to Israel! Death to America!"

"Not yet," Rafa commanded, pushing an errant strand of hair back up under the headband of her hijab. "Today we will send Israel a special present to remember the anniversary of their illegal nation. Look." Lying on the ground were a half-dozen kites. Homemade, three times the size of household toys, each sported a tail of twisted cordage thirty feet long that terminated in a bundle of rags tightly wrapped with wire.

"Do we soak the cloth in petrol?" one of the adolescent terror-trainees inquired.

"No," Rafa corrected. "It would burn too quickly, dropping the special present before it is delivered to the Jews. The rags contain charcoal. We soak it in lighter fluid and ignite it just before releasing it. That way, even if some coals spill out, the glowing chunks will burst into flame as they fall. Now, who is brave, and who is strong, and who is ready to attack the occupiers?"

Dozens of hands shot up! They might not yet carry AK automatic weapons or be dispatched through tunnels to knife Jews as they slept, but today they would strike a blow!

Once lit, the charcoal burned in tidy bundles. The kites, hoisted upright in teenaged fists, strained at the lines as if as eager as their handlers.

CHAPTER 2

"Now!" Rafa ordered. "Pull!"

Six lines of boys yanked the destructive toys into the breeze. The stronger winds aloft swept the kites higher and higher, until they emerged from the swirling smoke like wrathful dragons.

Rafa liked that image. She could use it in future recruiting efforts. 'Dragon-handlers.' That phrase would be useful in attracting ever-younger school children to the terror effort.

The flaming bundles had been spotted by the Israeli soldiers. If the kites soared successfully and dropped their blazing payloads into the grain fields and dry grasslands of southwest Israel, they could cause swaths of destruction out of all proportion to their unsophisticated appearance.

Tear gas shells arced toward the protestors, but as Rafa predicted, they fell short, and the noxious gas streamed back toward the Jewish soldiers. Rafa's charges laughed and jeered, even as bullets began zipping past them.

All the kites were launched. Now it was time to create propaganda targeting the inhuman Jews and their disregard for innocent life. Rafa held her cell phone up to her ear and pretended to receive a call. "What? What's that?" Holding up a palm in an imperious demand for silence, her cheering boys waited expectantly. "Already? Then we should move now! Immediately!" She addressed her recruits: "Our brave forces have already breached the hated Jewish prison fence. Thousands of our jihad warriors are pouring into the occupied land! Will we let them bear all this burden alone? Will we stay here in safety while they offer up their lives for us?"

"No! No!" croaking, still-changing male voices replied.

"Then go!" Rafa said, releasing them to charge the fence . . . and the Israeli gunfire. This day of 'peaceful protest' would become a major success yet.

3

The temperature was climbing as Jack passed through the strict security checks, surrendered his cell phone, and entered the headquarters of the Israel Security Agency, *Shabak.*

A balding civil servant in a short sleeve white shirt and no tie greeted him by name on the other side of the barrier. He escorted Jack to an elevator, pushed the down button. At the bottom level, he strode ahead through a labyrinth of windowless corridors. The ultimate destination was an unmarked, starkly modern office where a graying, uniformed Israeli officer with vivid blue eyes and a bandaged nose sat behind an empty desk.

The officer extended his hand but did not rise.

"Mr. Garrison." He motioned for Jack to sit. Noticing Jack's gaze, he touched his bandaged nose. "Skin cancer." Then he shrugged. "Glad you are here."

"Did I have a choice?"

"Not really, I suppose."

"They took my cell phone."

"Yes. Not permitted. The walls are impenetrable. Even the Prime Minister himself does not carry a cell phone."

"Well, who am I that anyone would want my cell phone? And who are you?"

"My name is Uri." The man leaned back in his chair and observed Jack for a moment. "I'll get to the point, Jack. May I call you Jack?"

"Yes."

"It seems you have some connection to one of Israel's most valued treasures."

Jack challenged. "And what might that be?"

"Not what. But who. You are the grandson of Dodi Baruch."

Jack laughed. "Well, yes. To my great surprise and joy. We have found one another again."

"Found. An interesting word. It might surprise you to learn that you were never lost. We have known the connection for some time. You see, your grandmother is an extraordinary woman. In our history she is the stuff of legends . . . only the legends are all true."

"I'm just beginning to learn the facts. There's been

a lifetime of silence about our Jewish roots within my family."

"You clearly have much to learn."

"Yes. And you have brought me here, why?"

"Your grandparents have, for many years, had a security detail assigned to them. Protection. They agreed to all of it. Upon the condition that it would not extend to security cameras inside the house, and that their privacy would not be disturbed." Waving toward a blue-enamel wall plaque displaying Hebrew words in raised white letters, Uri said, "Our motto: *Magen veLo Yera'e* . . . the Unseen shield. Of course, when Sol was alive, he was in regular contact. But Dodi is an artist. She would have nothing to do with it. You know what a victory it would be if, even at this age, your grandmother could be taken out by Islamic terrorists?"

"I hadn't thought of it. A woman of her age?"

"Age makes no difference. Except perhaps it has made her more stubborn. But she is a national treasure. We had hoped to put an agent in the house with her, however . . . "

"She refuses?"

"Exactly."

"And?"

"We are in hopes you might consider."

"Living with her? She hasn't asked me."

"In fact, we have inquired, and she tells us that you are the only person she would consider."

Jack squirmed in the fake leather, vinyl-covered seat.

"I'm an academic, not a warrior."

"You're an American. Second Amendment." Uri grinned. "You are a member of the NRA. College competition and medals in marksmanship."

"Years ago. You know a lot. So you also know I wasn't very good."

"Yes, we know. But you have demonstrated you can handle yourself in a crisis. We'll have to get you some additional training."

"I travel a lot. I can't . . . "

"Don't worry. It won't curtail your freedom. She also has a housekeeper."

"Housekeeper?"

"Who has other duties as well," Uri added quickly. "So. You will always have a backup. Always. We believe it would be a great benefit for you to live there. At least for a while. Especially now."

"I haven't agreed to this."

"You won't say no, will you?" Uri steepled his fingers, fixed his eyes on Jack, and waited for the reply.

"Alright, then. I am counting on that training, and not just who to call in an emergency. And backup."

"Excellent!" Opening a bottom drawer, Uri removed an Israeli-made pistol and slid it across the desk to Jack. "So, a Jericho 941. And, welcome to *Shin Bet.*"

✡ ✡ ✡

Omar remained in the lengthening afternoon shadows of an alleyway less than a block from the entrance to Dodi's home. Before Jack arrived at her gate, Omar observed the old woman's art gallery was closed and shuttered in advance of approaching Shabbat. The stone house that was the residence of an Israeli heroine was a veritable fortress. Cameras were set discretely around the high walls and gates of the property.

It took an expert to recognize the extent of impenetrable security the Israeli government had provided the artist and her husband, both of whom had been vital players in the establishment of Israel. Sol had been among the Jews who saved Jewish Jerusalem in 1948, and then had been a part of the brigade that recaptured the Old City from Jordan in 1967. Sol Baruch and his wife were among the first Jews to rebuild and move back into the Old City neighborhood that had been forbidden to all Jews for almost twenty years until the 1967 war. As such, the couple had been on the death lists of Palestinian hit squads for many years.

Omar scanned the stone buildings flanking the narrow lane. No doubt, there was at least one Jewish security officer stationed nearby to keep watch over Dodi's safety.

For having betrayed the Palestinian cause in Europe, and because of his later actions, the old lady's grandson had been added to the target list. It was assumed he also came beneath the protective wing of the Israeli Security

Agency, *Shin Bet*.

None of which disturbed Omar at all. As an ambitious member of Palestinian Islamic Jihad, Omar wanted to conduct complicated operations that would get him noticed and promoted.

"Highest priority," he had been instructed. "No safety for prominent Israelis nor for high profile foreigners. The world must see the resistance of the Palestinian people to Israeli apartheid again. And if no Jew is safe, the fearful will accede to our demands."

Targeted assassinations were also a way to undermine the PIJ's competitors, the Palestinian Authority and Hamas. Both quasi-government groups played at peace talk games with the Jews. Neither accomplished anything meaningful, especially when all true believers knew that only the complete destruction of Israel would meet the need.

Wheels-within-wheels, Omar thought. *How will a double killing reflect on that old Fatah bumbler Mahmoud Abbas? How will the Americans react? How will this undermine any peace talks and halt that nonsense of letting Israel call Jerusalem its capital? How would Omar's successful attack be received by the PIJ's biggest ally, Hezbollah? And how would it resonate with the Iranians who held the purse strings of terror?*

Omar shook his head. Stepping back around a further corner, he struck a match with his thumbnail and lit a Marlboro. The Palestinian brand named 'Liberty' was much cheaper, but they tasted like sawdust. Omar was glad he only had to concentrate on killing. Weighing and judging political ins-and-outs made his head hurt.

He made his way to a street café and took a seat facing the stone house and the art gallery. He sipped his strong Turkish coffee slowly and pretended to study a copy of Fodor's *Jerusalem*.

✿ ✿ ✿

The evocative scent of Jack's grandmother's paints mingled with the aroma of the star jasmine vine beside the gate. It smelled like home to Jack. For the first time since Debbie had died, Jack felt like he *was* home. Hefting his one duffle and ringing the bell, he inhaled oils, acrylics, and jasmine. Glancing at the security camera, he wondered who was observing his arrival at the entry of this living national treasure.

A buzzer sounded, signaling the all clear. The latch clicked, and Dodi's voice called to him, "Come in, Jack!"

Closing the wrought iron gate behind him, he crossed the courtyard, opened the door, and stepped across the threshold into her world, part of which was now his new residence.

Palette balanced on her arm, Dodi stood at the easel and contemplated a new still life in its beginning stages. She glanced toward Jack and smiled gently.

"You're late," she remarked.

He glanced at his watch. "I'm early," he corrected.

"I mean I've been waiting for my grandson to walk through that door most of my life. It's grand."

"That's as grand a welcome as I've ever had."

"And as true." She turned away from her work. "Take your bag back to your bedroom. Second door to the right. There is a WC and a shower adjoining your room. I'll make tea."

Knowing the house was as secure as a fortress, Jack passed beneath the arched doorway and walked down a corridor lined with framed family photographs. Captured within the old sepia tones were the faces of men and women whom Jack had never met, and yet they were familiar. Prewar Paris. Rome. A mountaintop in Switzerland. Smiling families and couples posing for the camera. In those happy years of the 1920s and early '30s, they could not have known the danger that pursued them, no matter where they traveled.

He paused before a photograph of young Dodi and her first husband, Jacob, Jack's grandfather, standing on the bank of the Seine with Notre Dame in the background. Then another shot of his grandparents holding a baby at a train station. Jack's mother?

Jacob looked so much like his grandson that for a moment, Jack felt he was seeing himself . . . before he was born.

Jack was torn out of his thoughts by the sound of the teakettle whistle. The sound was enough to wake the dead, just like the train departure signal at Paris's Gare du Nord.

Dodi's voice called to him, "Come along, Jack! Tea's on and shortbread biscuits . . . cookies as the American's say. Lots of time to get acquainted with your family."

Jack tossed his suitcase on the bed, splashed cool water on his face, and returned to the great room where Dodi sat curled in her massive armchair. A red teapot steamed on a tray beside a heaping plate of British shortbread cut in the shape of Scottie dogs.

He sat opposite her and held up a cookie with a questioning look.

"Walker's shortbread. I bought them just for you. I may be your grandmother, but that doesn't mean I bake cookies. Nor am I much of a cook. I may be French, but I never learned. I *can* boil an egg though. Can you cook, Jack?"

"Not well."

"Proof we are related."

"I do like to eat." He popped the Scottie into his mouth.

"So do I. So many wonderful cafes in our neighborhood."

"Then we're saved."

"When Sol and I married, and sometime later bought this house, I told him we must be good neighbors and support our neighbors' businesses. And our neighbors are almost all café owners and coffee house owners and the like."

Jack resisted the urge to ask her if she knew which of her neighbors were also *Shin Bet* assigned to protect her?

Dodi read his thoughts. "And there are a few unseen angels watching over us as well. I am the only gallery owner."

"And a treasure to Israel, I am told."

"If fighting and surviving and growing old make one a treasure, then I will simply say I represent all those heroes who did not live to see this moment in Jerusalem. At heart, I am really just your grandmother."

"And what should I call you?"

"What?"

"You are my grandmother. What should I call you? You like French? Grand-mere?"

"So formal. I'm Israeli now. Purely. I am a grandmother of no other nationality."

"I looked up a few of the Jewish terms. Safta. Or Bubbe perhaps? Or Nono, which is Sephardic?"

"Or perhaps you just call me Dodi?"

"Dodi suits me."

"Yes. I like the uniqueness of it." She winked and poured his tea. "Dodi. And I shall call you Jack because you are Jack . . . my grandson. But, if sometimes I perhaps slip and call you Jacob, it is only because you look so very much like your grandfather at the same age. And your grandfather never had a chance to live beyond your age, you know. So, Jack. Here you are. A miracle. As if you have stepped out of an old photograph. You have emerged from a vision. Frozen in time, when I parted from my beloved for the last time for this lifetime. And here you are, so very needed by me and welcome in this old woman's life. You. An amazing blessing, Jack, even if you can't cook. We will get along well."

Jack ate another Scottie cookie. "Yes. And Dodi . . . while I am here, would you tell me everything you can about those years? There's so much I want to know."

"I will tell you this, Jack. Our story is the story of six million others. Jews like us. We thought what happened in Europe could never happen. When the horror became a reality, we were simply too late. Our baby, your mother, was safe in America. But as for us, we were too late. The shadow of the long, dark night stretched over us. Many never awoke from the nightmare of those years. Jacob did not survive. I was one of the lucky few."

"And you came here and fought for Israel."

"I did what I could. We all did."

"You and Sol."

"We were very unlikely soldiers. A musician and an artist. But we did what we could. The Egyptians could go back to Egypt. The Syrians could go back to Syria. We Jews had nowhere to go but into the sea. With such a choice we thought we might as well fight. So we did. And a great miracle happened here, like in the days of the Maccabees. Israel not only survived but we who were artists and musicians and bank tellers and cooks and tailors; we took back the land from enemies whose only goal in life is to destroy us. Now *that* victory is surely proof of the hand of God. The God of Abraham, Isaac, and Jacob. The God of Israel."

"An unprecedented miracle."

Dodi agreed. "Unexpected. By anyone."

"And here we are. I'm glad."

"Better late than never." She glanced at the clock. "Yes. Well. What shall we have for dinner tonight, Jack?"

"Are you cooking, or shall I?"

"Nothing in the fridge. I'm afraid we'll have to go out to eat. I know a lovely place. A short walk from here . . . "

Jack had quickly become accustomed to the weight of the weapon concealed in his waistband. He took Dodi's arm, and they made their way up the twisting cobbled lane, aware that he walked beside a national treasure. He resisted the urge to smile up at the security cameras where the unseen *Shin Bet* angels watched over them.

✡ ✡ ✡

An hour had passed before the old woman and her grandson emerged from the gate. They stood a moment, scanned the lane, then slowly made their way in the opposite direction from Omar's position. He knew they remained within full view of Israeli security.

"Not today," Omar whispered, finishing his coffee and closing the book.

But the opportunity would undoubtedly come. One misstep, and they would come within range of his blade.

———————————————— ✡ ✡ ✡ ————————————————

The last rays of sunset streamed through the windows and lit the sacred fires of angels and saints depicted on the easels of Dodi's studio.

"I love the light in this room." The old woman laid aside her pallet and brush and directed Jack to sit. "Sol replaced stone walls with glass so I could create here. Windows for me. Sunlight and color."

Jack sighed and stretched his lanky legs out on a paint-spattered ottoman. The people in Dodi's paintings all seemed to be looking at him. Intense and holy gazes searched his soul. "There is a demand for honesty in their expressions."

"Ah, yes. Their eyes make us look inward. Inward. Truth in our own hearts."

Jack focused on the painting of Boaz meeting Ruth, illuminated by moonlight, on the threshing floor. The eyes of the man fixed upon her with astonishment at her beauty.

"Mother used to take me to the galleries. She would say that changing light is proof of art that is truly anointed by God. Our deepest longings. One instant of illuminated truth. The search for love. The quest for Eden."

Wiping her hands on a linseed-oil rag, Dodi nodded. "I have always been surprised by what the Holy Spirit paints by my hand."

"I am glad to hear you say that. I sometimes wondered if you are really of this earth. I mean, that you could see such visions, and then put them on canvas."

Dodi waved away the compliment with the scrap of cloth. "Not by me. But God gives me glimpses of what was. Moments . . . like snapshots . . . from thousands of years before cameras existed." She smiled at Jack, "Of course, you understand what I mean, don't you, Jack?"

"Visions," he confirmed. Not that long before this moment, it would have been an impossible admission. Now, here with Dodi, it made perfect sense.

"Yes," she concurred. "The eyes of a prophet see deeply into scripture's past. In those visions, he also sees the future. Even if only dimly."

Jack studied the image of golden wheat piled on the threshing floor of Boaz. "I come here to your studio, and when I see them all brought to life, it's as if there is no conflict in Jerusalem. Everything is accomplished. The chaff swept off to the side."

"Everything is seen."

"Everything means something?"

"Yes. You are truly my grandson. Everything has meaning. Even our suffering. Our threshing. It separates all that is useless in our lives. The hand of God will perfect us in our suffering."

"What was. What is now. What will be."

"Something like that. Yes. It is all already accomplished in the mind of our All-Knowing God. Heaven is waiting. We are almost home."

Jack sat in silence for a long moment as Dodi cleaned her brushes. He studied the wonder of Boaz, and could almost step into the moment; the realization of Love. He inhaled the aroma of oil paints and linseed.

At last Dodi sighed, "So, Jack, there is something else you want to talk about?"

He chuckled. "Yes: Bette. Her family. Something no one seems to want to talk about."

"Tomorrow is soon enough. Yes, I think tomorrow. Good night, dear Jack."

Jerusalem was quiet now. Dodi slept just down the hall
from Jack's room. He lay there, wide-awake, gazing at the
patch of sky through his high window. The stars began to
fade as the gibbous moon rose slowly like a billowing sail
on the eastern horizon.

Moonlight poured out liquid silver on the ancient land.
The same moon that had shone down on Boaz and Ruth
as they fell in love on the threshing floor of Bethlehem.
Jack wondered if Bette was awake in her hospital room.
Did she see the moonlight and think of him?

A shadowed figure stepped from the dark corner of the
room.

"Jack." Eliyahu's voice suggested amusement.

"I'm awake." Jack sat up in bed. "I was hoping you would come. So many questions."

"Ah, yes. Your thoughts were heard when you looked at your grandmother's painting."

"Just one man and a woman meeting on a threshing floor. A beautiful story. Worthy of moonlight and music too. But it's all a giant puzzle."

"It is written in the book. Every life, and every love story, is a part of the eternal picture."

"Ruth and Boaz. A love story. Clearly, love was not meant for me. How do I fit? Where do I fit?"

Eliyahu sat down across from Jack. The prophet's eyes studied Jack with the compassion of a father for a grieving son. "You must step back before you see the meaning of the picture. You live in a time when everything written is nearly complete. Yet you are here to complete the visions, you are a piece of the puzzle. The woman you love is also in this picture. Like Ruth, she has lost almost everyone. Everything. She, like Ruth, is afraid to love."

"But why?"

"Of all men, you should know. True love can bring great pain."

Jack nodded. "But to live without love . . . without her? When my wife died, I wanted to die. Then Bette came into my life. I saw the painting tonight and I thought, in the end, the story of Ruth and Boaz is just a love story. Why does it matter in the bigger scope of God's plan?"

Eliyahu replied, "It matters because the grief of these two lonely people was seen by the Almighty. Ruth and Boaz came from different lands. And yet they met. They fell in love. They married. They had a son named Obed, who had a son named Jesse. And Jesse was the father of a shepherd boy born in Bethlehem. That boy was named David. David, who became the King of Israel. The son of David was Solomon, who built the great Temple. Just there, where the moonlight shines tonight, Abraham offered Isaac as a sacrifice. Through their love and their lineage, Jesus the Messiah was born to bring salvation to the world."

"More than a love story."

"So you see the bigger picture? It is the greatest love story of all time."

"And how, with my small, sad life, do I fit into the puzzle? How does Bette fit?"

"You have both been to the threshing floor. You will see the fullness of your part in the story when everything is complete."

Eliyahu stood and began to fade into the light.

"Will you return?"

"Sleep now." Eliyahu's voice was a whisper. "What was. What is. What will be. All one story. Soon all will become clear."

———————————— ✡ ✡ ✡ ————————————

The teakettle whistled shrilly. Dodi set delicate floral china cups and a heaping plate of apricot thumbprint cookies and French pastries on the table before Jack.

He tasted a cookie and smiled. "Something from the pastry shop at Harrods, in London."

"I wish I made them," she laughed.

Jack took another bite and closed his eyes savoring. "Yes. Edible art. But more to the point, I have been waiting my entire life to taste my grandmother's cookies."

"And I have been waiting my whole life to make cookies for a grandson. I bought them, so they are mine! Dreams fulfilled."

She poured the tea and sat across from him.

"Yes. At last," Jack agreed. "There is so much I need to know."

She spread her hands in a very French gesture. "And so?"

"What do you know about Bette Deekman's family?"

"What do *you* know?"

"She told me she has a huge family here in Israel. But no one has come to visit her at the hospital. I mean, other than colleagues. Just me, mostly."

Dodi stirred honey into her steaming brew. "She told you she had a huge family?"

"A cousin of Wonder Woman, she said. Gal Gadot."

"Ah. Well. Our beautiful Bette does have a huge family. Every Jew in Israel is her family. Cousins without number, you see. We are all descended from two common ancestors. Abraham and Sarah."

"I'm talking about her immediate family. Her mother and father. Brothers and sisters. In Singapore on business, she said, but they could have been here by now. She talks about her mother. I think her mother should be here."

Dodi raised her index finger in a signal that indicated it was time for Jack to listen.

"Okay. What am I missing?" He fell silent.

"Did you notice an armed sentry outside her door at the hospital?"

"Yes. On duty outside the ward."

"He is there specifically for Bette."

"What do you mean? Why does she need protection?"

"Because she can't defend herself."

"Defend herself from what?"

"The question is, 'From whom?' The danger is much bigger and much more personal than you can imagine."

"But you also have protection."

"For different reasons. There are only a few of us remaining after the 1967 war who still need angels to watch over us. A few, like Bette, are the target of a very old personal vendetta. A *Fatwah* was placed against Bette's family after World War II."

"Seventy years ago?"

"Islam has a long memory. In some cases, many centuries may pass before revenge is exacted. Evil is persistent. Evil is patient."

"But seventy years?"

Dodi smiled slightly and narrowed her eyes. "Don't you know that the date of the 9/11 attack was chosen to commemorate . . . and Avenge . . . the anniversary of a great Islamic defeat?"

Jack shook his head. "Not a random date? 9/11/2001?"

"Not random. In 1683, a massive Muslim army marched to the very gates of Vienna. Christian kings from across Europe banded their armies together to fight. The date of the Battle of Vienna and the defeat of Islam is September 11, 1683. If the Christians had not been victorious, every cathedral in Europe would be a mosque. So, in 2001, the attack on New York was an anniversary. Part two of the battle. It was just the opening volley to a new Holy War."

Jack sat back and considered how much was new information to him. "I don't even know how much I don't know."

"We have a saying. 'Everything means something.'"

"But now you're telling me Bette's family has been a target for seventy years. Why?"

"Her grandfather was witness to a war crime. The son of a great rabbi, he was the lone survivor of the slaughter of an entire community of Jews. Later wounded, he climbed out of a mass grave in Hungary. He survived to testify against Muslims who worked beside the Nazi murderers. He also testified at the Nuremburg trials."

"So Bette's family has been under an Islamic sentence of death?"

Dodi nodded. "Yes. As I said, hatred is not just an emotion. Evil is a living *thing*. It grows and changes. It is a creature that opposes God. Evil exists and inhabits men. It seeks to destroy every Jew and every true Christian because we are the People of God's Covenant. Bette's grandfather and his descendants are Levites. They have a great and holy destiny for the nation of Israel."

Jack studied his grandmother's expression. Leaning close, he shook his head. "What is this about?"

"Jack, the *Fatwah* was never revoked. No matter what Bette told you about her family, every member has been targeted and killed. Executed, for want of a better word. Only Bette and one young brother remain alive."

Dodi sighed, drew a deep breath, and rubbed her forehead. "I also testified on Day Forty-Four of the Nuremburg trials. It was 1946. Even then, I still hoped your grandfather had survived. I hoped he was somewhere in a DP Camp . . . a Displaced Person's Camp . . . perhaps on Cyprus. That's where the British put survivors who wanted to come here. You see, the British still ruled this territory, and they were terrified the Arabs would revolt if they let Jews in."

Retrieving the faded black-and-white photograph from

the side table, Jack studied the picture of his grandparents when they were young and in Paris. Before . . .

"But he wasn't there? How did you find out?"

"There were lists. Not so many at first, but over time. The Red Cross made lists of survivors. Jacob Louzada was not on the lists of the living. Then, later, another list. His name was among those who had been killed. So I knew."

"What did you do?"

"I wrote Sol. Here in Jerusalem. I had made myself available to testify at the trials because I had witnessed so much. So much . . . " Dodi's voice trailed away.

Jack did not ask. He waited for her to speak or not to speak. Sun shone on painted angel wings. How was it possible that one woman, witness to such horror and brutality, could go on with life, creating such beauty out of the ashes?

Dodi said quietly. "So. Day Forty-Four, I testified. I sat in the courtroom among the murderers who killed the love of my life. I gave witness against them."

"You don't need to tell me," Jack said.

"But my story is your story. And it is, in the end, the story of Israel. Justice. It is why there must be an Israel. So we can say, 'Never Again.' And, 'Never Forget.' And I think if I do not tell you, Jack, you will not be able to repeat these things with any real conviction."

Jack reached for her artist's hands, and cradled them in his own. "Then tell me."

"Are you strong enough to step into my memory?"

"Yes. I'm your grandson. Strong enough, I think."

"Well then, here is what I testified. Auschwitz. We speak the word, and it is only history. But it was a real place and what happened . . . actually happened. I worked in the seamstress unit. We were directly across from the rail line and the gas chambers . . . separated by a fence, of course . . . but a clear view. I saw when the cattle cars rolled in. Filled with people, young and old. I saw when the doors were opened, and people came out, so afraid. And you know what I remember?" She paused as the memory came too-fresh. Tears flowed from her eyes and filled the furrows on her cheeks.

Jack gently squeezed her hands. "It's okay. You don't have to go on."

"But I must, now." Bracing her shoulders, Dodi resumed. "So. What do I remember? People. Goodbyes. I watched the people. My people. Jews from all over Europe. Ordinary people . . . like anyone. Families. Men and women. Mothers holding the hands of small children. Old couples married maybe fifty years, holding hands . . . just like anyone. And there was the gas chamber in front of them. They were being sorted. Who would live and who would die?"

Again, Dodi paused and inhaled deeply. "Do you know, I think they seemed almost as if they didn't think about it, that they were going to die. They cared only that they were being separated from one another. There was an old man and an old woman clinging to one another. They were torn apart, reaching, trying to hold on. And the Nazi guards enjoyed inflicting such pain. There was a barbed wire fence between my building and the tracks. I watched it all. Young, healthy, teenaged girls separated to the right. Their mothers and small brothers and sisters to the left were herded off to the slaughter. But, the condemned gave no thought to the fact that they were going to die. The gas chamber and immediate death held less terror for them than separation from their loved ones. Saying goodbye was the greatest pain. Most horrific. And I knew this. I knew because I had come by the same rail as they . . . but I had survived."

Jack nodded. "So they knew they were condemned."

"Everyone knew. Yes. We all knew. And the smoke from the crematorium rose high, and then ashes fell on all the surrounding countryside. Housewives dusted the ashes of those terrible farewells from their kitchen tables. Farmers plowed people into their fields. Turnips and cabbages grew in those ash-fertilized furrows. From the threshing floors of the Reich, the precious grain of Jewish lives was ground into flour. No one could say they didn't know. Those who deny the holocaust now and seek the destruction of Israel hope still to finish what Hitler began."

"And so you testified."

"Yes. Day Forty-Four. Yes. My testimony is in the

record. You could find it, I'm sure. The Nazis heard me. And I told about the night we were awakened by such terrible screams. Beyond description. We whispered in our barracks and asked what could this be? The next morning we heard what had happened. It seems they had run out of gas for the chamber. And so the *SS* simply threw the children alive into the fires."

Dodi looked away, as though she heard it all again. "And when I finished, the Nazi leaders responsible were executed. But many had escaped. Vendettas were sealed, and revenge promised, by the Nazi survivors against those of us who testified. The authorities changed my name and sent me here."

Jack offered, "In America, it's called a witness protection program."

"Sometimes it works. Bette's family was discovered. As for me, I have never been back. I loved Paris when Jacob and I were young. Such a beautiful city. If only we had left Paris in time. Ah, well, I am someone else now." She gestured at the canvases that surrounded her. "This is my world. Israel is my home. And now . . . you are my family."

"And yet you're still not safe," Jack muttered as he considered the security cameras which surrounded Dodi's home and neighborhood.

"But now it is for my actions in the 1967 War of Independence. As I said, *Evil* has a long memory. It is patient. It loves revenge against those who reveal its existence. *Evil* hates the Jews because we also have a long memory; because we are proof that God's promises are eternal. In the end, *Evil* will fall and never rise again. Meanwhile and forever, Israel still lives."

As much as Jack longed for better understanding . . . for answers to his questions . . . it seemed clear replies were not going to be immediately offered.

Mordechai Weissman clasped his hands on his desk and studied Jack. "That's the problem with you Americans: you think everything is about you . . . but it's not."

Jack shrugged. "I'm just trying to get the full picture here."

"What is left to tell? Bette Deekmann was assigned to protect you. She did her job well, and it almost cost her life."

"There's more going on here."

"What do you mean?"

"My grandmother told me as much as she could. She said you would know the rest."

"Knowing does not mean telling everything I know."

"Bette's Grandfather. Nuremberg. The *Fatwah* against him and his family?"

"Sounds like Dodi shared all the pertinent details."

"Enough. Except: *what* happened? What happened to Bette's family?"

There was a long pause. "Alright. The short version only. A quiet Shabbat in an Israeli village near the border with Gaza. A family of nine. Bette's parents, two brothers and a sister. The baby brother, the one who survived the massacre, was asleep upstairs. Bette's aunt was there with her husband and their children as well. Three Palestinians broke in, and within minutes, everyone was murdered. The terrorists left their footprints in the blood."

"They were caught?"

"No, unfortunately. Even after all these years, they have not been brought to justice."

"Go on. What happened?"

"So much blood there was no place to walk which was not covered with blood. And on the table was a calling card. On it was written the name of Bette's grandfather and the date of his testimony against the Nazis, and this threat, '*Inshallah*, to the Jews of the family of David ben Elijah, to the last generation. We will kill you from the eldest to the youngest. We will smash the brains of your infants against the wall, and we will finish what Hitler began.'"

"Where was Bette?"

"Driving back from reserve duty with the IDF. She arrived home to ambulances and police cars. They did not realize who she was. She was in her IDF uniform, you see. Looked official. She went inside." The supervisor opened his desk drawer and removed a file. He nudged it toward Jack. "This is what she found. This is what she saw."

Jack hesitated a moment, then opened the file. An involuntary gasp escaped as he looked down at the tangled gore of Bette's slaughtered family. Their blood covered the tile floor an inch deep and splattered the walls and every surface. On the refrigerator beneath cheerful family photographs held by magnets was a large swastika scrawled in blood.

"Poor girl. Poor Bette."

"Understatement."

"Yes."

"She identified her family members where they lay. Mother, father, siblings, the rest . . . and then she saw the baby was missing. She ran upstairs and found him. Found him still asleep. Imagine! She picked him up from his crib and carried him out the front door. The baby never knew; never saw. Never even passed through the hellish slaughter which was in that ordinary little kitchen."

Jack nodded curtly and closed the file without looking

at the other photographs. One glance was enough. He put his head back and closed his eyes. "I'm so sorry."

"Her brother still doesn't know. Bette decided to give him up for adoption. She's right, I think, and no one knows the youngest wasn't also killed. Better that way. For his safety, and ultimately, his emotional health. He's out of reach of the *Fatwah*. So she is alone, and has preferred it that way."

"I know I can't fully understand, but it does explain some things."

"This is what the people of Israel face, you see. Bette's family is only one family, but we Israelis are all under sentence of death by these animals. The world thinks World War II ended the racism, the hatred, the killing. And in all we still face, the UN condemns *Israel?* I tell you that Evil still lives. The war of annihilation against the Jews has never even paused to take a breath."

"What now?"

"This event brings up so much for her. Post-Traumatic Stress. So now, everything going forward must be Bette's choice, and in her own time. She fell in love with you, you know. Against her better judgment. And against policy."

"I know. And I love her."

"Well, she's a strong woman. Strong. Courageous. But I want you to know, my friend; I don't know many who could endure what she has endured and still go on."

"How can I help?"

"My opinion? Give her the distance and the time she needs to heal." Weissman slipped the file back into his desk. "As for yourself? Jack Garrison, be always aware. Watch your back."

✡ ✡ ✡

There were pieces to Bette's puzzle that Jack needed to put together. *Needed* was not too strong a word. He obsessed. He ached for her self-imposed aloneness. He longed to understand her reasons for staying away from her brother.

Maybe, he reasoned, if he *saw* the boy.

Was it possible?

Jack contacted Bette's commander with the question. Within an hour, Jack was on the road with Lev, back to the town of Ariel and the home of Lon Silver.

It was mid-morning when Lev turned onto the dirt road south of Route 5.

"A lot of changes in a year since we first came, eh?" Lev commented to Jack.

"Yes." Jack gazed out the window at the burgeoning sea of grapevines. "I am not the same man I was then." He paused. "Who would imagine I would come to love this land so much? My heart was stony ground. It seems like another lifetime. Like someone else."

"God does that. He softens hearts of stone."

The road to Lon Silver's vineyard home was familiar.

The town of Ariel sprawled across the once barren Samaritan hills. Jack remembered this was a part of the territory captured from Jordan by Israel in the Six Day War.

In 1978, Lon had asked the Israeli military for land that could be developed as defensible positions against assault. The city of Ariel, the 'Lion,' had grown from forty families and now had a thriving population of eighteen thousand Israelis. The surrounding land, once rocky and desolate, now bloomed with olive trees and vineyards.

In the year since Jack had first visited, the spindly new vine he had planted was green and flourishing in the midst of a thousand other vines. Jack remembered that first visit well. The cheerful embrace of Lon Silver and cigars all around for Lev, Amir, and Jack. Yet Lon had treated Bette differently. He had called her "Officer Deekmann." Rather than an embrace of welcome, he bowed slightly to Bette, shook her hand, and treated her with an air of respect due to royalty.

So, what was that about?

Jack hoped this meeting with Lon and his wife Dorith would shed more light on the mystery of Bette's life.

Lon Silver's modest house was set in the midst of several other homes grouped together for mutual security within the outlying agricultural community. Agricultural equipment sheds and long rows of greenhouses were nearby, all encircled by a wire fence set with alarms in case of attack.

CHAPTER 5

A dozen children played soccer in front of the house as Lon and Dorith sipped coffee on the porch and cheered them on. A bright pink bougainvillea bush climbed the sunny side of the dwelling. Pink, blue, and white petunias dripped from hanging baskets on the eaves.

A red-haired boy about eight years of age grabbed up the soccer ball and frowned at the intrusion of the automobile as Lev approached. The kids stepped back. Their expressions warned Lev that he dare not park in the middle of the soccer game.

Lon and Dorith grinned and waved a friendly greeting.

Approaching the car, Lon embraced Lev and Jack with his familiar bear hug.

"Shalom! Shalom! Come on! Come on! Have a seat!"

Dorith likewise embraced them. "I'll bring the cups. Coffee's fresh!"

The game reorganized and began again as a heaping plate of pastries and strong black coffee was set out for the adults. Lon's unlit cigar lay in an ashtray beside his cup.

"Neighborhood kids?" Jack asked.

"Our grandchildren," Dorith laughed. "Part of our tribe."

"This is only the soccer team." Lon rubbed the stubble on his cheek. "We have eighteen grandkids in all. Six kids of our own. Three kids each. Our quiver is full of arrows."

Jack scanned the faces, physical features, and honey-colored hair of the tribe. Plain to see they were

Silver offspring; all except the one carrot-topped kid in the rugby shirt.

Dorith followed Jack's gaze to the boy who was goalie at the near end of the field. "And how is Officer Deekmann?" She asked quietly, topping off Jack's coffee.

"Recovering." Jack replied cautiously.

Lon interjected, "Some things are hard to recover from." He seized the cigar, flicked a match with a thumbnail, and puffed the cigar into life. After studying the glowing ember, he jabbed it toward the soccer teams. "The wounds of a broken heart are much harder to heal than physical wounds. You know this."

Jack nodded. The image of the graves of his wife and their child in London came into his mind in a rush. "Yes. I . . . understand loss. The loss of everything dear to me. My wife and our baby were killed in a car crash three years ago."

"I'm sorry." Dorith reached for his hand and stroked it gently.

Lon added, "Then you understand Officer Deekmann's wounds, perhaps?"

Jack cleared his throat in an attempt to speak, but no words formed.

Lev pressed his lips together. "Jack was told some of the story. And that perhaps you could shed some light on . . . everything."

Lon raised one shoulder in a shrug. "If you know the details of the massacre, then perhaps it is enough that you are here; that you can see our grandson Benjamin there with his cousins. He is the goalie with the red hair, eh?"

There was no need to say more. The boy was Bette's brother. Strange, except for the color of his hair, he was a true match to her features. The eight-year-old blocked a kick and raised his hands in victory. Benjamin's laugh was the echo of Bette's laugh.

Jack frowned. "I see. Yes. Yes."

Dorith raised her eyebrows. "He is a happy child. Truly. One of ours. He doesn't know, but he is starting to ask questions."

Lon added, "It must be tough for Bette."

Dorith explained. "She comes sometimes. Always when she comes, it is in an official capacity. She keeps her emotional distance in every way. Formal. For his sake. We call her Officer Deekmann. He doesn't even notice her. Her decision, not ours."

"A wise and courageous woman. Selfless," Lon concluded.

They sat in contemplative silence as the soccer game was punctuated with happy voices. At last Lon stood. "Well, gentlemen, would you like to see how well your vines are growing since last you were with us?"

✧ ✧ ✧

Shabbat ended at sunset on Saturday, and the streets of Jerusalem came alive. The art gallery was just wrapping up Dodi's *meet-the-artist* reception. Coffee and pastries were almost gone.

Dodi, a half dozen art books beside her, was still seated in a red leather, wing-backed chair as Jack entered.

Royalty, was the word that came to Jack's mind.

Her bodyguard stood nearby. To the untrained eye, he looked like any other customer, but Jack spotted him immediately. The two men exchanged looks, indicating the event had been calm . . . always a relief when tourists packed a small area.

Dodi had been autographing art books for two hours. The crowd had thinned until only one couple remained. She chatted with British tourists from London and looked as though she needed to be rescued.

The old woman glanced toward Jack and beckoned. "And here he is now. My grandson Jack." Dodi was cheerful, but Jack could see the weariness in her eyes. "Jack! These dear people are from London. Mr. and Mrs. Goldman. Mr. Goldman works for the railway. I was just telling them that you would probably have a lot in common."

"I lived in Little Venice for several years." Jack shook hands.

Goldman tapped his chest with his thumb and replied, "West Hampstead. Agamemnon road. And London isn't what it once was, I can tell you. Remember the days when you could step onto a zebra crossing without fear you would be run over?"

"Good old days," Jack remarked absently as the shop began to close.

"No more. No more. Gone are the days. And Edgeware Road might as well be Pakistan. Not an English street sign or British shopkeeper to be found. Brexit! That's what I'm talking about! Brexit!"

Talking politics was a minefield that would be sure to keep Jack trapped for hours. "You know what I miss about England?" Jack took the fellow by his elbow and began walking him and his wife toward the door. "I miss the *patisseries*. Lemon tarts most of all. We had a devil of a time finding pastries for tonight's occasion."

"Yes. But the EU has laid down regulations for cheese making. Me and the missus are ready to retire and move out of London. Devonshire, where it's quiet."

"Nothing like English cows, I always say. Can't improve on Devonshire clotted cream." Out the door and onto the cobbles, Jack shook the man's hand again. "Thank you so much for stopping by! I know my grandmother appreciated your visit. Do come again. Cheers."

With a quick about-face, Jack reentered the gallery, closed the door, and locked it. He pulled the shade. Done.

Dodi leaned her head back on the throne, sighed, and then laughed. "I'm getting too old for this."

"Me too," muttered the bodyguard.

Dodi thanked the staff, and then led the way through

the back door into the main house. She was exuberant. "Oh, Jack! You did that so beautifully. They were here all evening. Multiple trips to the pastry table and drank so much coffee, I wondered how they could hold it. At least they bought two books to carry home to West Hampstead. We did very well. Three tourist's vans. Four entire crates autographed. A great success.

"Put the kettle on, dear. There's *baklava* in the box on the counter. And tell me all the news."

Jack stirred his tea and shared what he had learned about Bette's brother in Ariel. "Somehow I think it's too much of a burden for her. Living without any family. Denying that connection with her brother."

Dodi was silent for a long moment. "Perhaps if you had lived through what she lived through?" Dodi's personal memories seemed to hang like a shadow over her for a moment. "Unless you *know*, you cannot *know*. It is a great sacrifice for her. But she will do whatever she has to do to protect him."

"I can't help thinking that perhaps privately . . . I mean, if they could acknowledge one another quietly. In a way that would keep them safe . . . "

Dodi looked past him in thought. "The boy carries a great heritage. And with that, perhaps a great destiny. Only a handful of people know who he is; who his great-grandfather was. One day, of course, he must know. But perhaps only when he's a bit older. And only when Bette feels it is right."

The Russian-born Israeli sentry outside the door of Bette's
hospital room shifted his Uzi and practiced his broken
English on Jack. "Shabbat Shalom, Dr. Garrison. Bette
better. Out of ICU, eh?"

"Your English is sounding good today, Avner."

"I am follow your wisdom, pard-ner. Watch John
Wayne movies on YouTube to learn."

"With Russian sub-titles?"

"Yup."

"Well then, no bad guys will get past you."

Avner laughed, fell suddenly silent, thought about it a
moment, then laughed again. "Nope."

Bette was sleeping when Jack pressed the code pad, and

the lock clicked. He entered quietly. Sunlight through the slats of the hospital window shades cast shadows like the bars of a prison cell across Bette's crisp sheets.

He sat beside her and waited. Her thick hair was braided and draped over her shoulders like a little girl. Vulnerable, Jack thought, as he studied her face and the flutter of her lashes.

She sensed his presence and opened her eyes. "Shalom," she whispered.

"Shalom. You're very fetching this morning."

"Fetching?"

"An old English word. Charles Dickens. Beautiful. Sweet. Appealing. Alluring."

"All that?"

"In one word. At one glance."

"And I have another word to describe myself."

"Yes?"

"Desperate. Does it show?"

"No. But I'm not surprised."

"You know this place is a lot like being in prison."

"They're concerned for your safety, Bette."

"Right. Well, I suppose you know already, but the Commander tells me I'm being transferred to a secure site in Tel Aviv for Physical Therapy."

Jack had not known the details, but he had suspected she would not be staying in the hospital much longer. "I didn't know, but it makes sense."

Bette pressed her lips together and looked toward the light. "I miss my cat. I miss my house."

"They tell me everything is being taken care of."

"And Jack . . . I will miss you."

"Me? I'm more faithful than your cat. I'll always be here."

"No, Jack. Listen to me. I've had a lot of time to think about it, and I think it's best for us. At least for now. I need a little time, you see. I am not safe. Not a safe person for anyone to be around."

He took her hand and leaned to kiss her. She turned her face away. "I'm not going to accept this," he protested.

"It's a matter of you staying alive. I trained to take care of myself. You? You're an American professor who forgets to look twice before crossing the street. You will get yourself killed if you stay with me. And . . . and . . . look . . . "

"What are you talking about?"

"I'm talking about this. What happened to me?"

"I'm a liability?"

"To my safety? Yes. Until I'm well. Yes, you are. I need to just get well without wondering if you are going to step between a knife and me. I can't take care of us both, Jack. The Commander said . . . he *says* . . . and he's right. No room for falling in love."

"Too late."

"Haven't we both been to enough funerals for one

lifetime?" She pulled her hand away. "You're going to have to accept this because this is just the way it's got to be. I can't protect you."

Jack leaned back in his chair. "I've never left you."

"Well, you should have. You don't know . . . everything."

"Why did you make up that crazy story about Gal Gadot? And your big family? Why didn't you tell me about your family and your little brother?"

Her eyes brimmed. "None of that is your business. None of it. Like a lot of people in Israel, I have lost everyone dear to me."

"But you have a brother!"

"I haven't seen Benny as my brother in years. He's safe. He's someone else now. Not my brother anymore. But he's alive."

"You could have told me, Bette." Jack poured water over the ice chips.

"I don't speak of it to anyone. My little brother, you know, he was too young to know the details. He's a happy, normal, Israeli kid growing up with a good family. I see him sometimes, but he doesn't know I'm his sister. He doesn't remember anything."

"So what about you, Bette?"

"What about me?"

"You know what I mean. Are you going to avoid any emotional attachments from now on? Are you going to live out your life alone and *safe*?"

"Well, there it is, Jack. I've laid it all out on the table. It's not like I haven't had all this time to think it through."

He had a sick feeling in his stomach as she looked out the window at the patch of blue sky. "You know I love you," he said softly.

"You picked the wrong girl to fall in love with."

"Not my fault. It happened, and here I am."

She frowned and looked at the IV port in her hand. "Listen. Do you know the windows in this room are special? I can see out, but no one can see in. No tiny camera in a drone made to look like an insect can hover there outside and get my image. There's a coded lock on the door. I've got a bodyguard in the hall. Right now, inside these walls, I'm safe."

"I'm grateful."

She shook her head. "But very soon I will be well, and outside again, Jack. Sooner or later the enemies of my fathers will figure it out."

"You're saying this because of what happened. You took the guy out, and defending *me* almost cost *you* your life."

"I'm telling you this because it's *true*. I have been trained to take care of myself. I changed my name and identity after my family was executed. I'm always aware. I'm doing what I can. But here are the facts. The people who killed my family know that they missed my brother and me. But since then, my brother has disappeared . . . is off the radar. Me? I've been hiding in plain sight . . . living under their noses . . . and when I get out of here I won't have a guy with an Uzi sitting outside my door to protect me."

"Why do you stay here? In Israel, I mean."

"Israel is the safest place on earth for me. Security cameras on every corner. Look around you. We are all in the IDF, ready to go to war at any moment. Every Jew is under sentence of death by the jihadist Muslims, so we are aware. But for me, this is also *personal*. You don't understand how it works with our enemies. They do not forget, and they never forgive. There is a personal whisper of evil aimed against my bloodline. Like the eye of Sauron in *The Lord of the Rings*, you know. It sees me. And it will target anyone I love . . . whomever I love. If I let you love me, you will always be in danger too."

"If?"

"Yes. If."

"Well, you don't get to make that decision. Besides, it's already too late. I already love you. And you love me."

"Of course, I love you. And maybe I need to love you more. Love you enough to . . . "

"To do what?"

"To send you away. To step back. I don't know." Pleading, Bette raised her eyes to search his face. "I need time, Jack. I am in a safe place . . . but *I* am not a safe place. I need to heal, to feel strong again."

"Time? I want to marry you as soon as you can stand up. I want to take you far away from all of this, to the tallest mountain and . . . I was thinking of Wyoming." He gave a little laugh. "The least populated state in America. We could change our names. I could teach Social Studies in a high school, and you could open a martial arts studio for cowboys."

At last, she smiled. "Could I drive a pickup truck?"

"And ride a horse."

She sighed. "Oh, for such a quiet life. Oh, Jack."

"I'm only half kidding, you know. It's an American dream for sure."

"I can't let myself dream. No, Jack. Israel is my home. These people are my people. My family. I will never leave Israel."

"Okay, then. Time to think. And pray."

Sitting across from his grandmother with a pot of tea and a plate of scones, clotted cream, and apricot jam, Jack saw the family resemblance clearly.

As he looked into Dodi's golden eyes, he knew what his mother would have looked like if she had lived into her eighties.

"You look so much like Mom," he observed as he slathered jam on the scone.

"Rather, she looked like me, I think. Everyone said so when she was a baby." Dodi glanced away and smiled wistfully as if she could see a memory played out before her. "And you, of course, are so very much like your grandfather. Funny how connected the generations are, isn't it? Everything about you, Jack. Even the way you hold your butter knife."

"I would have liked to meet him."

"Look in the mirror. He'll be looking back at you. Like now. Through your eyes, he's looking at me over the years to this moment. Oh, the things we could not have known. It would have changed everything."

"I feel as though I'm home." Jack savored the tea.

"I worked for the British Mandatory government for a year," Dodi confided. "I acquired this habit. English tea served at 3:30." She leaned forward and winked. "I acquired other useful things from the British as well."

"Such as?"

"Blank visas, ID forms, and such for our people after they ran the immigration blockades. I would hand them off to Sol, and he would make certain they got into the right hands."

"So you were a spy?"

"I suppose I was. Yes."

"Would they have executed you if you had been caught?"

"The English executed quite a number of our boys. Palmach. Irgun. Yes. As for me, I was caught, tried, and put in prison."

"Prison?"

"Yes. Released the day Israel's Statehood was declared. May 14, 1948. The English prison guards fled the night of the thirteenth. Officers threw their keys on the desk and just vanished. We prisoners had no food for almost twenty-four hours. No news. None of us knew what was happening. Had the Arabs taken over? Would we be left to starve? Would we be taken out and shot? It could have gone either way."

"Were you afraid?"

"You stop being afraid when you have lived on the brink of annihilation for most of your life. You accept whatever may come."

Jack crossed his arms and studied the frail old woman across from him. Hard to imagine what she had lived through. "You are The Why."

"The why of Israel. The why of Hope. Yes. I shared a cell with a woman who was going to be deported back to France. She was a Jew who had fought with the Resistance against the Nazis. So she runs the British blockade, arrives in Eretz Israel to fight, and then is arrested. She roused the faint of heart among us. When the bombs began to explode, and dust from the cells rained down, she called out, 'Remember Joshua 3:5!'"

"What is that?"

"Our battle cry. Joshua told the people, '*Consecrate yourselves, for tomorrow the Lord will do amazing things among you.*' You see, after two thousand years of exile, we had only one more day to wait for the moment when Israel would live again! One more day to hope and the fulfillment of all things written in the Book would come to pass. So when we heard Egyptian planes, piloted by mercenary English pilots, above the prison, and old German bombs exploding in the prison yard, we prayed, and we sang Mitzvah Gedola." Dodi's voice quavered a bit, but still rang cleanly in the air as she burst into a scrap of song. "It is a great duty to always be happy, eh?" she translated. She refreshed their tea and smiled as though she was discussing bargains at a department store. "So, what else would you like to know?"

"Everything."

"There will be time for more stories. But now it's my turn to ask questions of my grandson, eh?"

"Alright. That's fair."

"So tell me about Bette Deekmann? How is she?"

"She was transferred to Tel Aviv for physical rehab."

"And?"

"She will be coming home to Jerusalem soon. Very soon."

"That's nice. Such a beautiful girl. She will be glad to be home, I'm sure. But what I'm asking, is, do you love her?"

Jack took another bite of scone and chewed thoughtfully. "I . . . it's still . . . well, I think about her. I think about her a lot."

"I bet you do." She laughed. "Well, all I have to say about that is, don't let the grass grow under your feet.

She'll be snapped up by some General before you know it."

"I haven't seen her since she was moved to Tel Aviv. She asked me not to come."

Dodi shrugged. "Wants to get back on her own feet without anyone looking over her shoulder, I suppose. I'm just telling you, Jack. That girl is a catch."

He nodded in agreement. "I'll see her soon. I'm hoping."

"Your grandfather, God rest his soul, knew he loved me the first time he saw me. And I loved him. But I needed a little space. Give her room. I think it's a good match, Jack."

"I have your approval then?"

"My blessing and my approval."

——————————————— ✧ ✧ ✧ ———————————————

Jack awoke with a start. At least, he thought he was awake. He was somewhere other than his bedroom, though, that much was clear. He seemed to be looking through a gauzy film.

The chamber in which he found himself featured a domed ceiling made of lime-washed stone. An arched doorway framed by tapestries of azure and turquoise and gold depicted river scenes of bulrushes and stalking birds. A single flickering lamp whispered messages in black, oily smoke to the unresponsive ceiling.

As his vision cleared, Jack saw he had a companion. He

was neither surprised nor alarmed to discover Eliyahu at his elbow. Nor were they alone. About two dozen grizzled men knelt in a semi-circle directly beneath the dome. On a gilded wooden bed in the center of the silent, watchful gathering lay a lone figure; gaunt and gray of complexion.

"The Patriarch, Joseph," Eliyahu remarked, gesturing to the recumbent man. "And those others are his brothers, sons, and grandsons. Listen."

"I am dying," Joseph said.

The voice that quavered with age was still strong enough to be clearly heard. "God will surely visit you, and bring you out of this land to the land He swore to Abraham, to Isaac, and to Jacob."

The dying man had once been the second most powerful figure in the lands ruled by the Pharaohs. The wall hangings were Egyptian, and on an ebony clothes rack hung robes spun of golden thread and the headdress of an Egyptian prince.

But Joseph had set aside the trappings of power; just as he set his sights on land beyond Egypt.

"Swear to me!" Joseph demanded of his kin. "Swear to me that you will carry my bones up from here. Bury me in the land promised by God and purchased by our father."

"We swear," the throng murmured.

Gold and turquoise, the fine clothes, and all the evidence of wealth swirled before Jack's eyes and disappeared. Suns rose and set. The moon paraded a thousand consecutive cycles like the twinkling of stars.

"There arose a new king who did not know Joseph," Eliyahu remarked.

They stood on a hill above restless waves. Beside them, facing the sea, stretched a caravan of Jewish families. Behind loomed a cloud that blocked the view; a cloud out of which darted tongues of fire.

Jack recognized Moses without being told. The Lawgiver stretched out his arms, lifting his rod of authority. When he raised his arms the winds blew, and the sea parted, rolling back on either hand like a scroll.

The children of Israel moved triumphantly forward.

Amid the procession was a coffin, born aloft by a dozen men. It was surrounded by a guard of honor carrying banners depicting a bull, a wild ox, and a jet-black flag with the image of a grapevine.

"He is going home," Eliyahu remarked. "He who was betrayed by his brothers, imprisoned after being falsely accused, who rose to power through his faithfulness to the Almighty, and saved his family and a nation from starvation. He is going home because of his utter confidence that God's promises to Abraham will be fulfilled when Israel takes possession of Canaan."

$$\text{———————————} \quad \text{✡ ✡ ✡} \quad \text{———————————}$$

Stronger than any image he had seen over the months, the vision of Joseph's funeral procession burned in Jack's thoughts.

He rang Lev before the sun was up. Lev's wife, Katy, answered in a drowsy voice, "Shalom, Jack. Do you know what time it is?"

"Hey, Katy. Sorry. Is Lev awake?"

"He is now. But I'm warning you, he hasn't had his coffee."

"I need to talk to him for a minute."

Jack heard her say as she handed the phone to Lev, "It's your crazy friend Jack. Open your eyes. He wants to take you to coffee."

The Old City of Jerusalem was just waking up as Jack and Lev sat in the quiet patio just outside Christ's Church. A few groups of jet-lagged pilgrims staggered past.

Jack inhaled the steam from his thick black coffee and watched the pre-dawn sky ripen into day.

"So you want to go to Joseph's Tomb?" Lev stirred cream and sugar into his cup. "Old Shechem is now called Nablus. Jacob's Well. Joseph's Tomb. It's where Abraham set up an altar."

"I need to see it."

"Shechem and The Way of the Patriarchs is now surrounded by one hundred and fifty thousand Muslims. It's one of the most contested locations in all Israel."

"Yes. I understand, but the Tomb of Joseph? Is there a more significant grave anywhere in the world?"

Lev gingerly sipped his brew and added another lump of sugar. "Violence against Jews is so common there. We have to get security clearance from the IDF to get in. And then groups of Jews can only come in about once a month. And only at night."

"What connections do you have?"

"Amir. He knows the ropes."

"Can he set something up?"

Lev nodded. "It's dangerous. Not a tourist destination. The Tomb of Joseph is God's deed to the land for us. Jacob bought it. Built an altar. Dug his well. Still there. And Joseph's children inherited it as their portion. And that's why it's so hated by the Arabs. It's proof that the patriarchs bought and paid for it. Proof that the children of Abraham, Isaac, and Jacob have had a legal deed for thousands of years."

"I understand." Jack leaned forward. "I truly do understand. Much more than you think."

"Okay, then. If you want to journey into the hornet's nest, I'll call Amir. We can hitch a ride with him."

✡ ✡ ✡

The multi-purpose room of the *Al Hoda* Kindergarten in Gaza was full of proud parents, expectant grandparents, supportive siblings, and various cousins. It was Graduation Day.

Rafa Husseini had been specially delegated by Hamas to attend today's festivities. *Al Hoda* school, whose name meant, 'The Guidance,' was operated by Palestinian Islamic Jihad. Hamas and the PIJ were frequent competitors for the allegiance of the Gazan Palestinians; competition that sometimes included denouncing the members of the rival faction as Israeli spies, or targeting them for assassination.

Rafa was not aware of any particular grudge Islamic Jihad had against her. Still, she had been accompanied on this excursion by two plain-clothes bodyguards. She selected a chair at an angle of the room where no one could approach her from behind, and she could keep an eye on both exits.

The walls were painted with slogans promoting the importance of education and Arab unity. Cartoon characters depicted smiling children wearing dress shirts and neckties while standing beneath a blue sky filled with white clouds.

It was all so . . . cheerful.

The center of the stage was occupied by the mockup of a stone building with a wooden plank door. A street sign, labeled in Hebrew, Arabic, and English, hung beside the door. It gave the imagined location, 'Al Quds Street;' Holy City Street, Jerusalem.

Jerusalem: the eternal and undivided capital of Palestine . . . or would be, when the Jews had been eliminated.

At a signal from the school principal, the audience grew hushed. A five-year-old, dressed in camouflage and a shape-obscuring ghillie suit, dashed up to the stage and threw himself down on it. The long barrel of the boy's toy sniper rifle covered the entry to the stone building.

He was joined on stage by four of his classmates. They wore camo uniforms and SWAT gear, and carried simulated automatic weapons. One of the 'soldiers' had a Palestinian flag flying from his backpack.

With the nonchalance of much practice, the four commandos surrounded the building, covering doors and windows. One of them pretended to toss something through an open shutter.

White smoke set-off on the stage began to billow up and out.

A nice touch, Rafa thought. Added to the realism.

At a signal from the leader, the Palestinian commando team burst into the building. They dragged out a school chum dressed as a member of the Israel Defense Forces and threw him . . . with considerable realism . . . to the ground.

One of the attacking children unrolled and displayed a banner over the prone Jewish soldier. "Israel has Fallen," it proclaimed in Arabic and Hebrew.

The audience expressed its appreciation with loud and sustained applause.

The largest of the child warriors emerged from the

building carrying a second target of the raid tossed over his shoulder, a schoolmate dressed as an Orthodox Jew.

The hostage taking a success, the leader calmly pretended to put a bullet in the head of the child portraying the Israeli soldier. The commando team withdrew as they had arrived: professionally, gravely, and silently.

A fresh burst of applause marked the end of the play, but it was not yet the end of the pageant.

All of the graduates, all wearing some form of warlike garb, and most carrying toy weapons, assembled on the stage in precise military formation.

As the audience members, including Rafa, rose to their feet, the children stood at attention. What followed was a speech recorded by Yasser Arafat, the last acknowledged leader of all the Palestinian factions . . . who had died a decade before the kindergartners had even been born.

"Well done," Rafa congratulated the principal.

"Please tell the children also," he urged. "They have been rehearsing for weeks."

"Of course I will," Rafa agreed. "In fact, I will let them in on a secret. Tonight is when the cowardly, infidel Jews sneak into Nablus. But tonight we have a special reception planned for them! I will tell the children that this memorable operation is in their honor."

8

The sun had set when Jack and Lev met Amir just outside Jaffa Gate. The Arab associate of Partners With Zion pulled to the curb and grinned, motioning for them to hurry and get in.

"Your timing is fortunate. Jews are only allowed into Shechem once a month. We're following a van carrying a small group of *yeshiva* students," Amir remarked as he pulled into traffic. "Our own little convoy . . . "

Amir was full of answers to unasked questions. "Nablus: modern-day Shechem is thirty miles north of Jerusalem in the West Bank. It is located between Mount Ebal and Mount Gerizim. Sound familiar?"

Lev interjected, "Deuteronomy 11. Moses gave the

instruction that when the people of Israel came into the land which God had given them to possess . . . from between those two mountains . . . they would be offered the blessing of serving the Lord or the curse of following after pagan gods."

Amir interjected, "Joshua shouted, '*Choose this day whom you will serve. As for me and my house, we will serve the Lord.*'"

Lev continued, "There's Joseph's Tomb, of course, and Joshua built another altar there . . . further laying claim to the land for Israel."

Amir rendezvoused with the unmarked Yeshiva van. "It was once a great center of Jewish learning." Lev gave a nervous laugh. "But now there are thousands of Jew-haters living there," he said. "Makes it difficult for Jews to go to Joseph's Tomb."

As they passed deeper into the West Bank, the red taillights of the students' van seemed like a warning beacon to Jack. He sensed the danger of unseen eyes watching their progress. "The air feels heavy here. Thick," he observed.

"We are entering into the territory of demonic strong-holds," Amir said. "But tonight the IDF will be protecting us, and the other Jewish worshippers."

Lev added, "Just getting to the tomb is an issue."

Amir gave a little laugh. "Did you see the dents in my car? Ah, well. I always say, what's a few Palestinian rocks chucked our way?"

"Well . . . thanks for the lift," Jack replied lamely.

Amir responded, "You're welcome, but I was coming anyway. Glad for the company."

The white twelve-passenger van of *yeshiva* students crept slowly through Nablus. A sullen mob of Muslim men lined the street leading to Joseph's Tomb. Amir, Jack, and Lev drove on the narrow lane at a safe distance behind the van.

"Who thought this was a good idea?" Lev muttered.

Amir worked the wheel of the dusty Toyota. "You worry too much, my friend. Just don't look frightened. They can smell fear. This was Biblical Shechem before it was Nablus. The enemies of Israel hate that fact."

Seen by the dim light of a flickering neon sign, Jack looked steadily into the face of a bearded man in a red-checked keffiyeh. The man spit toward the car. Jack returned a tight-lipped smile. "If looks could kill."

Amir rattled on. "Fear to them is like blood in the water to a shark. Trust me. Nothing will happen. Trust me. These guys hate Jews. They hate tourists. They hate living next to the Tomb of Joseph. They hate you. But I promise nothing violent will happen. The IDF would be on them like a duck on a bug."

Jack hoped Amir was right. Repeated acts of violence and vandalism were commonplace against the tomb and against Jews who came there to worship. Even in the gloom, Jack had never seen such hatred simmering in the expressions of the people who were just a few feet from where they passed. Jack's sense of spiritual darkness increased still more. It was as though they were moving through an oppressive, malevolent fog.

Lev prayed quietly and then remarked, "There are more angels with us than the number of demons who are with them."

At last, the floodlit compound of Joseph's Tomb came into view. Domed roof and high walls enclosed the Jewish holy site where the patriarch Joseph had been buried. Over recent years this sacred location had been attacked and desecrated by Muslims many times. A once thriving Jewish community had been driven out.

Inside the compound, Jack knew, IDF soldiers were on duty to protect the worshippers.

The van pulled up directly in front of the entry portal so the doors could swing open and the passengers could enter with the least exposure to danger. Jack felt intense relief, but that feeling of peace only lasted for a moment.

The gate opened. The *yeshiva* students began to disembark, but suddenly, as if by signal, the Muslim crowd erupted in ferocious fury.

"Allahu Akhbar!" came the shouts of hundreds of voices. A Molotov cocktail was flung high into the air. It crashed down, shattering against the exposed side of the van, which burst into flame. A dozen other homemade bombs were thrown, illuminating the night until the exterior of the vehicle was covered with liquid fire. A hail of stones followed, shattering its windows.

Lev shouted, "Punch it, Amir!"

Jack ducked as a rock smashed the rear window of their car. He saw there was no place to escape; nowhere to go but inside the compound.

Amir jammed his foot on the accelerator. The car lurched forward, scattering the crowd. Despite Amir's sharp wrench of the steering wheel, the Toyota slammed into the bumper of the burning van.

Fire licking the exterior of both vehicles provided a momentary shield between the compound entry and mob.

A dozen Jewish students tumbled from their bus and stampeded through the gate into safety. Enemy shots rang out, striking the Toyota.

"Get out! It's going to blow!" Lev warned. "Into the compound!"

Jack threw the car door open, but it banged against the wall. "Too close!" he shouted.

Amir threw the car into reverse, backed up, and wildly attempted to maneuver the vehicle to give them enough room to escape.

The extra seconds cost them . . . dearly. A bullet sliced through the roof, striking Amir in the neck and shoulder. He slumped forward onto the steering wheel. The horn bellowed like a wounded animal.

Amir's blood sprayed the inside of the windshield.

Jack managed to open his door and roll out onto the

ground. He reached up and tore at the driver's-side door handle. Grasping Amir's limp body, he pulled the man onto the ground and shouted, "Lev! Get out! Get out now!"

Lev tumbled out, crawled over Amir, and helped Jack drag him toward the safety of the compound.

The gate opened a fraction. Friendly hands reached out and pulled them inside. The gate was locked and bolted.

Outside, the roaring of "Death to Jews!" and "*Allahu Akhbar!*" drenched the air with maniacal fury.

Amir lay on the stones of the courtyard in a widening pool of blood. His eyes were open and staring.

There were shouts in Hebrew for help.

Two IDF medics, each wearing the red star of the *Magen David Adom,* rushed in, pushing Lev and Jack to the side. Working by flashlight, one squeezed a pressure point, while the other packed Amir's wound with a coagulant-filled dressing in an attempt to staunch the bleeding.

But it was too late.

"I'm sorry," said the medic after a few minutes. He shook his head. "There is nothing I can do."

✡ ✡ ✡

The death of Amir barely made the news outside the borders of Israel. There was a celebration in Gaza of course; the handing out of candy, and the burning of

American and Israeli flags.

But Amir was, to the rest of the world, just one more dead Israeli in a long list of dead Israelis. At best, the response was apathetic. At worst, there was a smug judgment that he deserved what he got for trespassing on hostile ground.

The incident passed almost unremarked. Amir was buried within a day.

Time to move on until next time.

After the funeral, in the patio of Christ Church with Lev, Jack stretched his long legs and leaned his head back. Their coffees were almost untouched; props used as an excuse to just sit there.

Neither man spoke for what seemed like a long time. The passing clouds sailed like an armada on the high winds above Jerusalem. A gentler breeze stirred flags below.

"What now?" Jack sighed.

"More. Always more."

"Why Joseph's Tomb? Why such immense hatred?"

"Why did you want to go there?" Lev asked. "What did you want to see?"

"I heard Joseph say, 'You must carry my bones up from this place. You must.' And he told them, 'God will come to your aid and take you out of Egypt to the land he promised on oath to Abraham, Isaac, and Jacob.' And then I saw the coffin of Joseph being carried through the Red Sea."

Lev nodded. "Right, Jack. That answers your question. The Tomb of Joseph in Shechem is proof that Joshua brought Joseph here and buried him in the land God gave Abraham on oath. The tomb is proof that God fulfilled his oath. And that is reason enough why the Arabs hate Joseph and the descendants of Abraham, Isaac, and Jacob so much."

"Attacks on the compound barely make the internet."

"And yet, if I were to pick the most significant holy site in Israel, after the Western Wall and the Temple Mount, I would say this is it."

"I'm sorry." A surge of remorse filled Jack. He thought if he hadn't insisted they go up to Shechem, Amir would still be alive.

Lev read the guilt in his face. "Get over that one. Amir was going to go anyway. You tried to save his life. They were ready for us when we came; gunning for us. It's the way it is up there."

"I just don't get it. I mean, no international outrage at this."

Lev picked up his coffee cup and took a sip. He made a face. "Lukewarm. Get my meaning?"

"Right."

"Let me show you something." Lev fiddled with his cell phone for a minute. "Here it is." He passed Jack the picture of a group of a dozen attackers, surrounded by smoke, waving a Palestinian flag on the dome of the tomb.

"This desecration was October 7, 2000. Tishri 8, 5761. Right in the middle of the High Holy Days. The same date, Tishri 8, in 948 B.C., there was a two-week-long celebration to dedicate Solomon's Temple. Significant. The 2000 attack on Joseph's Tomb barely made the news. It got a great big shrug from the Clinton administration. Not a word of condemnation. The day of that attack on Joseph's Tomb, I read this passage in the prophet Amos." He thumbed through his tattered Bible and pushed it across the table to Jack. "Go ahead; read the underlined verses out loud."

Jack traced the warning of Amos, beginning in chapter 6. "*Woe to you who are complacent in Zion . . . you notable men of the foremost nation to whom the people of Israel come . . .* "

Lev frowned. "Prophecy is all about patterns. Even though this scripture was applicable in the distant past, I knew when I read it there is only one country that 'the foremost nation' could mean; only one nation in the world the people of Israel could come to for help."

"The U.S." Jack pondered the words.

"Yes. And the warning says, 'Woe to you.' Read on. The underlined verses."

Jack cleared his throat, "*You put off the evil day and bring near the reign of terror. You lie on beds inlaid with ivory, and lounge on your couches. You dine on choice lambs and fattened calves. You strum away on your harps like David. You drink wine by the bowlful and use the finest lotions.*" Jack inhaled sharply at the words that followed. *"But you do not grieve over the ruin of Joseph."*

Jack raised his eyes. His gaze locked on Lev's stricken face.

Lev asked, "Are you getting this?" He took the open Bible from Jack.

Jack said, "The ruin of Joseph? This can only mean the destruction of Joseph's *Tomb*. Right? Am I right?"

"There's so much here. The consequences to those of the foremost nation who are apathetic about the destruction of Joseph's house. America." Lev began to read again. *"For the Lord has given the command, and He will smash the great house into pieces and the small house into bits . . . I will deliver up the city and everything in it."*

Jack came to it suddenly. He exhaled loudly and put his hand to his head. "A year later. The twin towers."

"Yes. 9/11. One week before the High Holy Days. In the month of Elul, the month of repentance. Before a year had passed since the destruction of Joseph's Tomb, this prophecy of Amos to the great nation came to pass. And as we all watched on television, both towers were smashed to bits. I watched men searching the rubble, and I read this . . . and I knew."

Tears stung Jack's eyes. "The world's indifference toward the destruction of Joseph's Tomb opened a spiritual gate which allowed evil to flood into the world. Into America."

"Yes." Lev nodded. "Yes. I have not shared this with

anyone 'til now. It's all there. Read closely. All of the destruction of the World Trade Center is described in chapter six. Searching for bodies: verse nine. Searching for survivors: verse ten. Calling for people to hush as they search so they might hear a voice call to them." Lev paused a moment and read again. "Chapter seven. 'Though they climb up to the heavens, from there I will bring them down.' So . . . "

"Connect the dots. The dedication of Solomon's Temple: 948 B.C. The year 2000: on that exact date, comes the desecration of Joseph's Tomb in the middle of the High Holy Days. Met by absolute apathy by the 'foremost nation' to whom the people of Israel go. And finally, within that same Jewish year comes the destruction of the twin towers."

PART II

9

Just a mile and a half south of the Partners With Zion office where Jack worked with Lev, was The Israel Museum. The institution housed one of the world's leading art and archaeology collections.

Without sharing his intentions with either Lev or Bette, Jack had made a personal commitment to learn all he could about the historical roots of his Jewish heritage as quickly as possible.

Starting with the museum seemed a great idea.

The entry fee included a special temporary exhibit dedicated to the Wars of the Maccabees. *That's something I know nothing about,* Jack thought.

Paintings had been brought to Jerusalem from

collections across Europe. Jack sat down on a black leather bench in front of a canvas by Peter Paul Rubens on loan from the Museum of Fine Arts in Nantes, France. The fictional portrait, entitled 'The Triumph of Judas Maccabeus,' was five feet tall and four wide.

Judah, a heroic figure portrayed in Roman cloak but medieval-era breastplate, stood over fallen foes, his eyes cast heavenward. Behind his right shoulder, the severed head of an enemy was held aloft on a spear. Beside Judah's extended right arm a bearded, hooded man like an Old Testament prophet, held a war hammer, symbolic of Judah's nickname and his reputation.

Background figures blew victorious blasts on curved trumpets. Plunder being looted from the litter of bodies was not pocketed by Judah's men, but was instead handed to older onlookers dressed as Jewish prophets or perhaps priests. Brush strokes of crimson and sable, steel and gold, flesh and earth, presented a moment frozen in time. Hands were outstretched. Shoulders were bowed with the burden of plunder. A horse, nostrils wide, reared away from the smell of the carnage.

Jack's gaze darted back toward the center of the painting. Judah was plainly the hero of the piece, but it was the blue-robed figure holding the war hammer that drew Jack's attention. The angle of the wooden shaft of the weapon seemed to have changed. The wrist of the holder appeared to pivot toward Jack as if extending the hammer to him.

And then the eyes of the figure hooded in navy blue met Jack's.

Recognition happened a split second after a fragment of terror.

It was Eliyahu . . . and this was another vision.

The museum disappeared. So did the painting and the aftermath of the battle. The Judean hill on which Jack and Eliyahu stood was bathed in dawn hues of dusty periwinkle and diffuse saffron. An east wind brought the scents of parched earth and crushed sage.

Jack's guide spoke as if they had already been in the middle of a conversation: "It was not enough for the People of God to be promised the land," he said. "They had to fight to possess it. Sometimes they had to fight to keep it; sometimes fight to recover it. Sometimes the sin that gave birth to judgment still required purification after repentance."

Jack shook his head. "I don't know enough to really understand."

"Follow me, then," Eliyahu instructed.

The hillside disappeared, and in its place was the Temple Mount. Jack recognized it from previous visions . . . yet, not as he had seen it before. There was a temple there, but it was neither the Temple built by King David's son, Solomon, nor the expanded structure of Jesus' era.

"We are two centuries before the birth of the Messiah," Eliyahu explained. "Judah has returned from its captivity in Babylon. The Temple has been rebuilt, but the people have merely exchanged one overlord for another. In place of the Babylonians and the Persians, now the land is fought over by the successors of Alexander the Greek. He is dead. His generals and their heirs have divided Alexander's conquest of Asia Minor from his triumph over Egypt."

"And the dividing line is right here in Judea," Jack ventured.

Eliyahu nodded. "Antiochus, the fourth king with that name, rules here now. He styles himself as Greek in religion and culture, and so all those who seek his favor do likewise. Look."

In open contradiction of the second Mosaic law prohibiting the worship of graven images, the courtyard in front of the Temple was dotted with statues. Jack recognized Poseidon by his trident-spear and Artemis with her bow.

"Filth and defilement everywhere," Jack heard a voice behind him say. Turning around Jack saw a pair of elderly male Jews. Their faces were imprinted with disgust and revulsion. The taller one spoke again. "I tell you, Lemuel, judgment is coming . . . and soon."

"Lower your voice, Micaiah," Lemuel said in rebuke. "We are surrounded by traitors who would like nothing better than to carry tales back to Antiochus."

"If I cannot speak what I feel, then I may vomit," Micaiah complained. "See?" A cadre of chanting, scarlet-robed priests led a pair of pigs toward the altar of sacrifice.

Lemuel and his friend lifted the hems of their robes off the defiled stones and hurried away.

"Inside the Temple now stands an abomination," Eliyahu instructed. "A statue of Olympian Zeus. Antiochus caused it to be carved so that his own features are recognizable on the face of the idol."

It sounded to Jack as if Eliyahu was near puking also.

"The king has instructed," Eliyahu continued, "that he is to be called *Epiphanes*: the god made manifest."

"No wonder the Orthodox Jews are so upset."

"The king has burned the Torah scrolls. It is death to possess one . . . death to teach Torah . . . death to circumcise children . . . death to keep the Sabbath. Antiochus has decided to stamp out the worship of the One, True God in one generation."

"So what happened?" Jack demanded.

"Come and see."

The Temple Mount was replaced with a rural village on a hillside dotted with olive trees. Small stone cottages flanked a central market square crowded with people.

"This is Modi'in," Eliyahu instructed. "A day's walk northwest of Jerusalem." Eliyahu gestured toward an imposing male with a long white beard, a great mane of hair, a high forehead, piercing eyes, and prominent cheekbones. The man reminded Jack of pictures he had seen of the American abolitionist John Brown.

"Mattathias the Hasmonean," Eliyahu instructed. "He is a hereditary Levite priest, but today he has refused to perform a sacrifice for his village. Antiochus has demanded all the villages of Judea prove their loyalty and obedience by sacrificing to him."

A carved wooden statue depicted Zeus seated on a throne. He held a scepter in his left hand. Some kind of angelic, winged messenger stood upright on his other palm. Jack guessed this idol was meant to be a portable duplicate of the abomination in the Jerusalem Temple.

The square thronged with villagers, but two lines of warriors prominently faced off across from each other. On one side, near an altar on which a fire was already blazing, was a red-robed priest. With him were ten soldiers with helmets, shields, and swords.

On the other side was Mattathias, and resembling him were equally stern-faced men from teenaged to mid-thirties. All imitated their father's pose, with their arms folded across their chests.

"Mattathias's sons," Eliyahu indicated. "Jonathan, Eleazar, Simon, John called 'Gaddi,' and . . . "

"Judah," Jack completed the sentence for his guide. "Next to his father. Not sure how the painter Rubens managed it, but he got a pretty fair likeness eighteen centuries after the fact."

"Do you still refuse to do your duty?" the court official demanded of Mattathias. "Three people of this village have already been executed for hiding scrolls and for circumcising their sons. I hoped you would help them learn obedience and save their lives."

"Have you not heard?" Mattathias returned. "*'You shall have no other gods before me,'* says the Lord. *'For I am a jealous God.'*"

"Yes, yes," the government official replied scornfully. "We know what your outlawed books say. But here and now is the law of Antiochus Epiphanes: You shall bow down and worship me." Approaching the altar, he summoned a servant to bring forward a goat for sacrifice.

It was at that moment that Mattathias and his sons struck. From under a fold of his robe, Mattathias drew a sword . . . Judah a steel-headed club . . . Jonathan a dagger. The youngest, Gaddi, produced a sling.

It was over in a moment. Mattathias killed the pagan official with a single swipe of his blade, while Judah crushed the skulls of three enemies. All the rest, some wounded, fled.

It was not entirely a triumph for the Hasmoneans, however.

"What have you done?" someone in the crowd cried out.

"They'll come back with the army and kill us all," another shouted. "Who gave you the right to drag the rest of us into this?"

Eliyahu touched Jack's arm, and the scene wavered

and faded. "Mattathias and his sons take to the hills," he explained. "As Antiochus grows more and more ruthless, they gather an army and train in hit-and-run warfare. When Mattathias dies, not many months after what we just saw, Judah becomes the commander of the Jewish forces."

✧ ✧ ✧

"Where are we now?" Jack asked. Pre-dawn twilight masked a broken landscape of bare limestone hills, dotted with wind-carved pillars and clumps of acacia.

"The Jewish rebellion has been underway for three years," Eliyahu explained. "There have been few pitched battles, but the skirmishes have mostly been Jewish victories. Lysias, Viceroy for Judea to King Antiochus, now leads an army of sixty thousand men. He expects to crush the Maccabees once and for all. Lysias has marched from his camp near Hebron toward Jerusalem, going to the aid of the Syrian soldiers holding the citadel in the Holy City. He knows Judah Maccabee has less than ten thousand soldiers. He thinks Judah will flee when he sees the size of the Syrian force."

The sun rose clear of the horizon, revealing more of the scene. The main road wound through a narrow defile, hemmed in on both sides by rocky cliffs. The mouth of the canyon, opening some mile or so to the south of Jack's location, displayed the mounded cottages of a small village.

From the direction of that settlement came a blast of trumpets and a thunderous hammering of drums. The Syrian army advanced toward the pass.

Behind every large boulder, sheltered from view by clumps of eight-branched sage, strung out along all the side-ravines, were Judah's men. Jack could not count them, but the Jews seemed vastly outnumbered by the host coming against them.

Lysias deployed his cavalry. *Five thousand strong*, Eliyahu murmured. The horsemen, eager for glory, galloped ahead, creating a gap in the order of march. Once inside the wadi, the cavalry was forced to slow down, hemmed into a space no more than a half dozen horses across.

Eliyahu lifted his hand. A long, bony finger pointed across the canyon. Arms folded across his chest, Judah Maccabee studied the enemy from the shadow of a wild olive tree growing from the cleft of a rock. The tension Jack felt increased as nothing happened. The wait was interminable.

Now the Syrian horsemen were three-quarters of a mile inside the ravine, and the first third of the infantry were well within its mouth.

At a gesture from Judah, a pair of men on either side of him raised ram's horns and blew loud, shrill blasts . . . signaling the call to launch the ambush. The ravine echoed and re-echoed with the sound as more and more trumpets repeated the challenge. Both ahead of the cavalry and in the space between the horsemen and the infantry, Judah's men levered huge piles of boulders down into the crevice, blocking either advance or retreat for the cavalry.

A volley of arrows and a hailstorm of slingstones hammered the Syrian troops. Horses reared and plunged, throwing and trampling their riders, making it impossible for Lysias' men to dismount and fight back.

It was a slaughter.

The line of foot soldiers, hearing the cries of anguish and alarm, also came under attack. Judah's men pelted them from the heights with rocks and spears. Any Syrian trooper who tried to draw a bow was instantly targeted from both sides of the ravine.

Lysias' men broke and attempted to flee, but were blocked from escape by their own forces. Jack saw Syrian soldiers hack at their comrades, trying to escape the rain of death. When at last there were no Syrian soldiers alive in the canyon, the remainder did not regroup in the village but continued in headlong flight toward the west.

Judah Maccabee's arms were once again folded across his chest. A look of grim satisfaction was on his bearded face.

"Lysias' men won't stop until they reach the seacoast," Eliyahu told Jack. "Five thousand Jewish warriors have killed five thousand of the enemy and put fifty-five thousand to flight."

"Is it over, then? Have I seen it all?"

Eliyahu shook his head. "Come with me. There is more to witness."

✡ ✡ ✡

Eliyahu inclined his head toward two strong young men, whose features glowed bronze in the firelight. They stood among the officers of the Jewish army and stretched out their hands to gather in the warmth of a watch fire.

Jack recognized Judah, and a family resemblance between the two men. "The brothers again. Plain to see."

"Judah the Hasmonean is now called: *Maccabee*, the hammer of Israel. *Aluf alufim.* Champion of champions. Commanding General. Not since King David was there such a great warrior in Israel as this man. And his brothers. At his side tonight, for the last time, is Judah's younger brother: Eleazar the Zealot."

The neighing of warhorses from the opposing camps echoed across the valley.

Jack asked, "You say this is the last time the brothers will be together. Will Judah die? Or Eleazar? Both?"

"Tomorrow this ragged band of Jews will face fifty thousand troops." The wizened prophet put a finger to his lips. "Listen," he instructed.

From the enemy camp came the trumpeting of elephants.

Eliyahu continued, "The feats of young Eleazar are

recorded in the books of the Maccabees." The prophet snapped his fingers. In an instant, the scene changed to dawn and the roar of terrible slaughter. "See there!" The prophet stretched his arm and pointed. "It's Eleazar!"

The young warrior was in the thick of the fight. Eleazar raised his head and slashed his way toward the largest of the enemy's beasts of war. Lumbering through the carnage, crushing any man in its path, a great elephant, its tusks bound with bronze bands, carried a Syrian commander forward into the fray.

Jack's horrified gaze followed the young Eleazar, covered in the gore of his opponents, as he fought through the throng, finally reaching the elephant. Arrows bounced off the creature's thick hide and armor sheathing. Eleazar shouted and raised his sword, then dove beneath the elephant! With a mighty thrust, he plunged his weapon into its belly up to the hilt. Intestines and blood spilled out. A terrible scream erupted from the beast as it faltered and fell . . . crushing Eleazar to death.

Eliyahu said, "This is how it ends for young Eleazar, but the Jewish army will survive to fight once more."

Again Eliyahu snapped his fingers and then it was night again. Jack and Eliyahu returned to watch the parting of the brothers by the campfire.

The two sons of Mattathias clasped arms. "Whatever comes tomorrow," Judah's voice quavered. "Whether we live or die, I know that we shall live! I know that Israel shall live and Jerusalem! . . . Jerusalem! The Temple of Solomon! . . . Jerusalem! The eternal capital of our people!"

Eleazar nodded and embraced his brother. "I am not afraid, Judah. I know that even though I die, I will live again, as it is promised! For this destiny, we are called to live! For this moment upon the threshing floor when all evil is winnowed out like chaff and scattered on the wind! Our time is now. What we do here will change the course of history. We are ordained by the spilling of our blood to fulfill the Eternal Promise."

Then slowly, Eleazar raised his face and peered directly at Jack. He narrowed his eyes and searched the shadows, then laid his hand on his sword hilt and frowned. "Who is that I see, brother?" Eleazar whispered. "I see in a mist, a man . . . no, two men, observing us in this very place, yet the one is far off. He watches us from a far distant time . . . "

Eliyahu inclined his head slightly, acknowledging Eleazar.

Judah replied, "Brother! I see nothing. No one in the shadows."

Jack grasped the sleeve of Eliyahu and whispered. "I thought they couldn't see us."

Eliyahu replied. "He cannot see us. He sees the shadow of what is to come. We see the past, and he sees the future. One carried the shadow of the other."

"There is no changing the past. I know that," Jack said.

"We can't warn him. Eleazar will die."

Taking Jack's arm, Eliyahu said. "The brothers who fought here are united now. They each gave their blood with all the others. Oh the cost! Such a great cost has been paid for the sake of Jerusalem! All the past is present in this land. And now the Lord, Himself, winnows the wheat from the chaff in this very place."

The watch fires of the opposing army covered the hills like fallen stars. A vast galaxy of sentinels waited for dawn and for death.

"Come, Jack," Eliyahu guided him. "It is time we return to Jerusalem."

✧ ✧ ✧

Once again, Jack and Eliyahu stood atop the Temple Mount in Jerusalem. An icy wind swept across the plateau. The narrow crescent of a waning moon hung overhead. Eliyahu led Jack to a perch above the Hinnom Valley. "Tell me what you see," he instructed.

A bonfire was kindled in the depth of the canyon. Against the glare of the leaping orange flames, Jack was at first horrified at what he thought were human forms in the blaze. A moment later, he realized, "Statues," he said. "Burning the idols."

"On the garbage heap known as *Gai Hinnom* . . . Gehenna," Eliyahu agreed. "The Temple Mount has been

cleared of all pagan worship. The entire structure . . .
inside and out . . . has been washed and scrubbed and
washed again. Tonight marks the exact third anniversary of the abomination. It is the twenty-fifth day of
Kislev. Since the Jewish victory at Beth Zur, which you
witnessed, Jerusalem has been firmly in the hands of Judah
Maccabee. Listen to Judah praying."

Judah Maccabee, still in battle dress, stood in the
middle of the Temple plaza surrounded by hundreds of
his men. *"O Lord, we have cleaned this place holy to the worship of
Your Name. We have torn down the defiled altar and built it anew of
unhewn stones. We have restored the menorah and the altar of incense,
the table of the holy bread, the veils and the gates. Now we beseech
You: May the heroes who fell for their loyalty to You and to the land,
who fell to liberate the Temple and the Temple Mount and Jerusalem,
Your Holy City, be under Your divine wings. May their place be rest
in paradise, and may they receive their allotted portion at the End of
Days. Amen!"*

Like a mist is dispelled by a passing breeze, so the
image of the Jewish soldiers at prayer wavered, parted, and
drifted away. Once again, the plateau was empty of people.

Eliyahu said, "The cleaning and purifying has been
going on for some time. It was in Judah's mind to dedicate
tonight to rekindle the divine worship of the Almighty . . .
but there's a problem."

"I know about this," Jack offered. "It takes a week to
create purified oil for the holy menorah, but there's only

enough sacred oil for one night."

Eliyahu's countless wrinkles crinkled into a hundred tiny smiles. "So you have been studying," he said with approval. "And what is the result?"

"The Miracle of the Oil," Jack reported. "That single jar of oil continued to supply the needs of the menorah for eight nights . . . long enough for the newly prepared holy oil to be ready for service. Just like . . . " Jack stopped as a sudden thought struck him.

"Yes?" Eliyahu prompted.

"Wasn't there a miracle connected with the Prophet Elijah?" Jack eyed Eliyahu before continuing. "A miracle in which a certain widow's flour and oil did not run out until the Lord sent rain to end the drought?"

Eliyahu nodded his approval. "Now returning to this Feast of Dedication. How do we celebrate this miracle?"

"Lighting one light on the first night of Hanukkah. Two on the second, and so on for eight nights."

"And what is the significance of these holy days? What is the message?"

Jack recognized that he must have progressed in his understanding of the visions. Instead of just being a witness and a beginner, now he was being tested on a deeper level of meaning. "It means when the Almighty approves of commitment to an action, He also provides the resources."

"Good. And?"

"A little light banishes the darkness?"

"There is no such thing as darkness overwhelming light," Eliyahu expanded. "When a lamp comes into a dark room, the room can neither comprehend nor oppose the coming of the light. Do you have more to observe?"

Jack pondered. It would have been easier and safer for the Maccabees and their followers to give into Antiochus' demands . . . weighing present threats from real soldiers against obedience to an unseen God, they chose the more difficult path. "Standing up for what's right, even if you are persecuted for it, is the right thing to do."

At the end of a tunnel of black night, gleamed a single oil lamp. The glowing beams pushed back the shadows. The shining orb grew and grew until it resolved itself into Rubens' portrait of Judah the Maccabee . . . and, Jack was once again seated on a leather-covered bench in a museum.

10

In the months since Bette had said goodbye, she had not answered one email from Jack. When he tried phoning, her cellphone went directly to voicemail that announced it was full and could take no more messages.

He felt as though her life had been spared, and yet, even so, he had lost her.

Dodi asked him over breakfast, "Have you heard from Bette?"

He shook his head. "No."

"Have you asked anyone about her?"

"She's okay. Physically okay, I hear. But I don't know what happened. Why she doesn't want to see me? Let alone talk to me?"

"Have you tried writing?"

"Her email is blocked. Texts blocked."

Dodi smiled with amused pity. "Oh, you children," she sighed. "Jack. I mean write . . . as in, write a love letter. Apply ink upon a sheet of paper. 'Having fun, wish you were here. I love you, and can't breathe without thinking of you.' That sort of thing? Have you?"

"Well, no."

Dodi shrugged. "Or just tell her you miss her. Old fashioned, yes. Give it a try. You never know what a postage stamp might lead to."

✧ ✧ ✧

Jack's letter lay open on the kitchen counter by the Keurig coffee machine.

His handwriting was a mysterious scrawl. She could not ignore it. The message took her a while to decode.

He wrote, "I miss my friend. It's an ache, Bette. Remember what Professor Higgins sang about Eliza? 'I've grown accustomed to her face . . . '"

"Eliza who? Professor Higgins?" Bette frowned at the writing then Googled the reference. Rex Harrison popped up, singing mournfully about Audrey Hepburn in 'My Fair Lady.'

Bette played the song on YouTube. "Oh," Bette said aloud to no one in particular as a pang of loneliness and pity surged through her. She reread Jack's cramped, painful, cursive. "I miss my friend."

"I miss you too, Jack," she whispered.

Bette's fifth-floor studio flat in Tel Aviv was neat, drab, and as generic as any chain hotel room. News on the flat-screen television kept her company.

She had a view of the crowded white sand beach along the aqua curve of the sea. Long solitary walks on the shore had strengthened her. Physical therapy was going well.

She rang Mordechai Weismann on his private cell. "I can't do this anymore," she declared.

"Bette. You're safe where you are. You've got the best view in Tel Aviv. Paid leave. What are you saying?"

"I'm saying . . . I'm saying, I miss my cat."

"Your cat?"

"I'm saying I miss my beautiful mess and the clutter of my Jerusalem flat. I'm saying I hate this sterile, safe, secure, too-neat, little shoe box. I'm saying I want to come home." She hesitated.

"And?"

"And I want a life. To get back to my life, messy as it might be. Whatever that means. I want what other people have. A life. You know?"

He laughed. "Doctors say you're not ready. Not back to full strength. Recuperation will take a while. You can't expect to come back on full duty."

"Whatever. Like I said, I miss my cat. Put that in my

file."

"It will take a couple weeks to get it all arranged."

"A couple weeks? I'll go nuts. Just tell me this. Can an inmate have visitors for lunch?"

"Your cat?"

"You know who I mean." She held up Jack's letter and waved it in the air at the cell phone.

"Your cat's name is Jack?"

"Stop."

"So it's the Professor, eh?"

"Yes, the Professor. I guess it is."

✧ ✧ ✧

The tide of pilgrims, tourists, and residents ebbed and flowed past the Jerusalem café, unremarked by the pair seated at the sidewalk table. Jack could not have answered whether the strangers numbered in the teens or thousands; his only focus was on the woman seated opposite him.

Reunited at last . . . sort of, but it was not a comfortable meeting. *She's here, but she's not here,* Jack thought.

"Bette? Something's up." Jack searched her chocolate brown eyes, hoping to find the reason for her remoteness. "There's something you're not telling me. Is there someone else in your life?"

A sad smile played on her lips. She glanced toward the crenelated walls of the Old City. "No," she replied with too much hesitation, a whisper of uncertainty.

"Your answer is not really an answer. Bette? Since you came back to Jerusalem from re-hab, you haven't really been here. I mean, *present*. With me. Like your heart is somewhere else." He reached across the table to touch her hand. She did not withdraw it, but neither did she respond.

"I have been thinking a lot about your life, Jack."

"*My* life?"

"Yes. Your wife. Your baby. How much you lost and, forgive me, how desperately bitter and unhappy you were when we first met."

"Yes. I know. Angry at everybody and everything. The world seemed so empty to me."

"What changed? The world is the same. So full of endless hate and turmoil. But you. You're a different guy. There is a light in your eyes. I wonder how that can be since the woman you loved is gone, and your whole life was turned upside down. I see tragedy and loss all the time here in Israel. We stand at the edge of the grave of someone killed so young or so uselessly, and I wonder . . . how do you get over that?"

"I found my faith again. Faith that God's real. And heaven is real. And all goodbyes are only temporary. Like parting at a train station and one day I will board the train, it will pull into heaven's station, and because she also believed, my wife and child will be waiting for me."

"Is there still room in this life for you to fall in love

again?"

"Bette, I have come to care for you deeply. Love you. Everything in my life is different now. But you seem to have pulled away from me. Something in you changed too."

"I don't know how to answer this, Jack. You know about my family . . . know more than almost anyone else in the world. And yes, something else is different. How could my life not be different after all that happened? I mean, yes. Something happened to me. A lot of things happened to me. In the first place, I almost died. Maybe I did die . . . I'm still trying to figure it out. The time I was unconscious . . . and yet . . . here. In this world, but not really in this world. Like your voice and the voices of the doctors were shadows. Like a dream to me."

"Okay. I get it. A sort of post-traumatic stress reaction?"

"Not exactly. But, yes, there's something that happened to me. But I'm not ready to talk about it because I can't sort it out, you see?"

"Not exactly. But I'm really trying."

They fell silent as the waiter came by and refilled their iced tea.

"Just be patient with me, Jack. Can you please be patient? This is a whole new world for me. I was all about my job for all my adult life. First, the IDF and then, security detail. I mean, I loved the daily challenge. The excitement. Now I get up every day, make coffee, and listen to the radio with the cat. And then I read what's going on instead of being part of it." She shrugged. "That's quite a change."

"Everything's different for me too, Bette. So I hear you."

She nodded. "You're somebody different than the cynical guy I first met, that's for sure. What happened to you?"

"You happened. And other things. Other things I may never be able to explain." The bells of some ancient church began to toll the hour. "This city is a time machine. A place where you can step in and out of the centuries and find yourself rounding a corner and suddenly coming face to face with . . . " He hesitated.

"With what?" Bette leaned forward and studied his face. "Tell me, Jack. Face-to-face with what?"

"Truth."

"History."

"There are ten thousand faces of history. A different interpretation of every event. But there can be only one Truth."

"Do you mean face-to-face with What is Truth? Or Who is Truth?"

"For me, the One Truth is Messiah. Yeshua. He called himself 'The Way, The Truth, and The Life.' He said, 'No one comes to the Father but through him.' And yes. I believe that truth."

Bette looked away. "Maybe. Maybe it is true. Maybe he is the truth. But I don't know. I have lived here my whole life, surrounded by people looking for the way, the truth, and the life. And this is the first I can say I'm seeking too."

"Please, Bette. Don't shut me out. Let's walk on this journey together."

They sat in brooding silence for a time.

"Here's an idea," Jack offered. "What would you think of a double date? At least, that's what we call it in the States."

"I know the phrase," Bette retorted. "Who and why?"

"Lev and Katy," Jack offered thoughtfully. "They seem to be getting it right, you know? And Lev's my go-to guy when I have questions . . . and I still have lots of questions about this new faith of mine."

Seeing a suspicious frown crease Bette's brow, Jack hurried on. "Not to lecture or convince you, never that! They're just nice folks and fun to be with. Shall we give it a try?"

There was a long pause while Jack held his breath.

At last Bette replied, "Sure. Why not?"

✦ ✦ ✦

The Jaffa restaurant was called The Old Man and the Sea, in Hebrew: *HaZaken VeHayam*. The table on the outdoor terrace was right beside the marina. An ice cube plucked from the freshly squeezed lemonade and tossed from where

Jack and Bette sat would have ricocheted off three fishing boats before splashing into the Mediterranean.

"Hemingway," Bette remarked, waving the menu. "The last novel published before his death."

"Pulitzer prize," Jack returned, in a spirit of friendly competition.

The cheerful, yellow sun beamed down out of a pristine blue sky, but nothing warmed Jack like Bette's smile as she continued, "When asked about the symbolism in the book Hemingway said, 'I tried to make a real old man, a real boy, a real fish, and real sharks. But if I made them good and true enough, they would mean many things.'"

Jack bowed and spread his hands in surrender. "I didn't know you spoke Hemingway."

"I learned to speak English reading Hemingway. If only he had written about Israel."

Jack and Bette were meeting Lev and his wife Katy for lunch. The two women had not yet met. "Tell me about Katy," Bette encouraged.

"Ah, Katy," Jack said. "She of the red hair! Irish. Talented fiddle player. Vivacious. Mother of four brilliant children. Truly much better than Lev deserves!" then he hastily added, "A situation Lev and I share!"

At that moment, Lev and his wife arrived. Katy's copper locks gleamed in the sun as they made their way to the table. Katy embraced Bette as if they had been friends forever. "Ah, didn't Lev say you reminded him of Wonder

Woman? But you're much prettier."

"Too kind. But I see Jack was telling the truth for once when he said you are a 'knock out.' You have pictures of your children?" Bette asked as they settled in.

"And what sort of mother would I be without pictures?"

A moment later Katy and Bette were engrossed in iPhone photos of the Seixas offspring. "The oldest three, no account wrestlers like their father . . . if ever they live so long," Katy explained. "Ah, but Brigit, she's my darlin'. Can't decide if she's a musician or a dancer . . . "

"Perhaps she'll be both," Bette said as she flicked to the next photo.

A pair of whirling dervishes transformed into white-apron-clad waiters. An impossibly large number of small plates of appetizers materialized as if by magic: carrots, beets, olives, falafel, cauliflower, mushrooms, hummus, and a mountain of pita bread. "But we haven't ordered yet," Jack protested.

Glancing at the women with their foreheads almost touching, Lev ripped off a chunk of bread and corrected, "I'd say, don't worry about it. Can't you already tell this is going to be a three-hour meal?"

An hour passed before the conversation turned serious. Jack explained, "With the renewed rise of anti-Semitism in the Christian church, Lev's mission is to connect pastors from all around the world with the fulfillment of Bible prophecy, which is the modern state of Israel."

"Seventy years since statehood," Lev noted.

Bette asked, "Prophetically significant?"

Lev replied, "Yes, and that's not the half of it. Just past fifty years since the recapture of the Old City and the Temple Mount."

"I understand the Biblical significance of a fifty-year-cycle," Bette interjected. "A year of jubilee. Freedom."

Lev continued, "Exactly. So all things converge. A hundred years since the Balfour Declaration, defining the need for a Jewish state. A hundred years since the British captured Jerusalem from the Turks in the First World War. So: fifty years from the end of Ottoman rule to the taking back of the Temple Mount. Another fifty years from then to 2017."

Jack whistled softly. "Like a continuous celebration. Punctuated by the U.S. moving into its Jerusalem embassy."

"One hundred and twenty years," Bette calculated, "since Theodor Herzl, the father of Zionism, organized the first Zionist Congress in Basel, Switzerland."

"One hundred twenty," Katy repeated. "Is that a significant number too?"

Further discussion paused while a waiter arrived with their lunch.

"Grilled chicken kebabs and the red mullet, fried, to share." Bette raised her glass. "A toast to celebrate this moment when all things converge."

Four glasses clinked.

Lev resumed. "One hundred twenty years is the length of time Noah was building the ark. One hundred twenty years from the beginning of the Zionist movement to the miraculous state we witness today." Lev gestured around them at the packed restaurant and the sea. "I put it to you," Lev said to Bette and Jack. "Would anyone argue with a comparison linking Israel and the absolute necessity of a Jewish homeland to Noah and the ark?"

Bette concluded. "The land of Israel. Our ark. And one more link, Moses, our deliverer, lived to be one hundred and twenty years. As a secular Jew, I always believed Israel as a safe homeland for Jews was enough."

Katy asked. "And now?"

Bette paused a long moment. "I admit it seems as though all prophecies lead to this moment in time. Religious Jews are saying the Messiah will come soon. There is so much here. I am listening, truly I am. But it is almost too much to take in at once. Much food . . . and much food for thought."

Katy put a hand on Bette's arm. "Of course. Almost too much at one sitting."

"I was born in Israel. My great-grandparents knew Hertzl personally, and were among the first to drain the swamps and plant orchards. My grandparents fought in the 1948 War of Independence. Sabras. But they were not religious. No. It was for the sake of Jewish survival that they did what they did in the land. Not to fulfill Biblical prophecy. I am not sure they were even aware of all this, you know?"

Lev nodded and passed the last of a platter of pickled cauliflower. "And yet they were the fulfillment. The beginning of all that is happening."

Bette shrugged and repeated. "I don't think they cared for any idea past the absolute necessity of a Jewish homeland. We may see a lot in hindsight today, but as Golda Meir often said, 'We Jews have a secret weapon in our struggle with the Arabs. We have no place else to go.'"

And so the three-hour lunch evolved effortlessly into four hours of conversation. They might have stayed long enough for supper too, and never wearied of the conversation. They parted as though they had known one another for a lifetime.

Bette held Jack's hand as they left the restaurant. Neither of them noticed the man at the bus stop on the opposite side of the street who had been waiting patiently for them the entire afternoon.

11

Partly sheltered inshore of a Tel Aviv breakwater, a score of preteen hopefuls were learning to surf. They were all dressed alike, matching black shorts with royal blue rash guard shirts. Their boards were a panoply of colors from scarlet to pink, purple, and gold. With serious and self-conscious concentration, Israeli youth wobbled atop one-foot-high Mediterranean waves.

"Reminds me of Lev and me," Jack murmured to Bette, seated beside him on the bench. "One Spring Break from Baylor, we went to Surfside Beach, Texas."

"So?" Bette returned. "How was it?"

"'Bout like this," Jack returned with a dismissive gesture. "Gulf of Mexico: surf is hot, salty, and boring.

But peaceful, you know? Like these kids. They act like any conflict is a million miles away."

"That is, after all," Bette said, "the goal. A nation where kids grow up without mortar fire falling on their schools, or worrying about knife attacks in shopping malls."

The sound of the waves gently lapping the shore made Jack drowsy. His head nodded toward his chest until the screech of a gull made him jerk himself awake. How had he slept so long? Why had Bette let him doze the day away? From mid-afternoon, the sun was now an orange blob on the horizon. And where had Bette gone?

The surfers were also gone. So too was the breakwater. The corpse of a decaying tramp steamer, its keel cracked and its hold open to the sea rotted just offshore.

"Here's your group leader coming now," someone said. "Call him 'Paris.' Shalom and good luck."

The figures of a dozen men coalesced around the dark green, wrought-iron bench on which Jack found himself, but gave no indication they were aware of him.

A vision or a dream, but this time there was no guide. Eliyahu was nowhere to be seen.

A gust of wind blew a scrap of newspaper against Jack's leg. The headline of the front page of The Palestine Post read, "Israeli Planes Bomb Capital of Trans-Jordan."

The date was 1948.

"All right, gather around and listen." The stocky young

man code-named 'Paris' was below medium height. He pushed a lock of curly brown hair out of his pale blue eyes and surveyed the ten middle-aged volunteers of the newly formed company.

By their dress, age, and manner, Jack categorized them. Three shop clerks, two bank tellers, four waiters, and maybe an undertaker? Evidently, all had been recruited from the businesses of Tel Aviv to help with some urgent need. It seemed all Paris could do to keep from sighing, but apparently, his job was to encourage, not to sow despair.

"You are about to be heroes," Paris said, "without ever firing a shot. Jerusalem is starving. The ration for each of her one hundred thousand people is six slices of bread . . . and even that will be gone by the day after tomorrow. You know the pass of Bab el Wad is controlled by the Arabs? Well, the *Palmachnik* boys figured out a jeep track connecting Jerusalem to here, and the road is being widened even as we speak."

Heads nodding, one of the bank tellers said, "So, you want us to drive jeeps? I can do that."

"No," Paris disagreed. "There aren't enough working jeeps in all Tel Aviv. No, you and I and three hundred like us are going to carry supplies over the last miles of trail that still can't take a truck . . . on foot."

A pair of fiftyish, narrow-shouldered, stoop-necked shop clerks exchanged a glance. Paris watched them stand up straighter and lift their chins.

"So what are we waiting for?" one asked.

Paris and his men, with Jack as an attentive observer, rode on dilapidated yellow school buses to an abandoned British army base marking the bottom of the supply route to Jerusalem. In the warehouse commissary, Jack watched as Paris and his company each received a tan canvas backpack stuffed with forty-five pounds of flour, sugar, and dried vegetables. At the starvation ration now available in the Holy City, each pack carried enough food to provide one hundred Jews one more day of life.

Temperatures on the unheated buses plummeted as they ascended the Judean hills. A chilly breeze swirled down from the heights. Coming from the Mediterranean shore, no one was dressed for cold.

Jack pondered what he was seeing. 1948. Jewish Jerusalem was starving. The 1948 War of Independence was reaching a crisis point. If Jerusalem could not be resupplied, then it would be lost. Calling the Holy City, 'the eternal, indivisible capital of the Jewish people,' would be an international joke. Jack needed no interpreter to define what the loss of Jerusalem would mean to Jewish morale. The fate of the infant nation of Israel hung in a tangle of resources, each suspended by a spider web of hope.

The line of buses crawled upward, gears clashing and engines laboring. The caravan climbed out of the gorge as it turned onto the narrowest of tracks.

Toward the north, across the dark expanse of Bab el Wad, a trio of flares erupted. Three signal rockets, two red and one blue, exploded in the night sky. All the Tel Aviv volunteers dove for the floor of the bus. At Jack's feet, a waiter, still wearing a white apron tied high up under his armpits, hugged the supply pack as if trying to hide behind it.

The flares were followed by the crump of mortar rounds, and a moment later by the crash of explosives . . . nowhere near the line of buses.

"You can get up," Paris remarked drily. "They have no idea where this road is. The Arab artillery fires blind when they think they hear something."

The interior of the bus was lit only by shielded flashlight and the green gleam of florescent watch dials. The dim glow was enough for Jack to witness conflicting emotions on each face, chagrin at appearing cowardly coupled with a reluctance to leave the perceived shelter of the floor.

"Anyway, there's no point in worrying about it," Paris remarked. Rapping his knuckles on the corrugated metal of the bus's body, he joked: "This wouldn't even stop a well-aimed rock."

Jack and the others heard the terminus of their travel before they reached it. A bellowing cough like an angry bull alerted them to the dozer carving out the highway of Jerusalem's salvation. In the wake of the grader, a score of men wielding picks and shovels straightened, broadened, and smoothed the new track.

"The Burma Road," Jack muttered to himself. "Nicknamed for the famous East Asian supply route in the Second World War."

"End of the line!" Paris ordered. "Everybody out. Quicker we get moving the sooner you get warm! This is why you came. Let's go!"

Paris organized his squad into a single file of men, each clinging to the shirttail of the one in front. "No lights!" he explained. "Can't give the Arabs a target, eh? I go first because I know the way. Everyone ready? Move out!"

Whether dream or vision, the hike was real enough and strenuous enough that Jack, like the others, was winded and straining within the first half mile. The supposed jeep trail was in places no more than a path for shepherds to drive their goats to market. The bare trace circled knobby hills, dipped into canyons, climbed out again around boulders, and scrambled over gravel patches that slipped underfoot. Every moment was another opportunity for a broken ankle . . . or a plunge over a ledge into an unseen finality.

After hours, it seemed, Paris halted the file of panting porters. "Five minutes rest," he said. "Here is water." He passed a canteen back along the row. "One swallow each, only."

The waiter who had clasped the pack on the floor of

the bus spoke up. "Captain Paris," he said, though the two words took three breaths to emerge from his throat. "I don't need . . . to rest. Why . . . are we stopping?"

Even without being able to see the look on Paris's face, Jack heard amusement in his reply, "Because from here on, the way gets steep."

This was no joke. When the hike began again, it was to attack a hillside vertical enough to be called a cliff anywhere else.

"Now you can let go of the shirttails," Paris ordered. "Some places you will need to use your hands. Knees, too! No shame in that. Don't trust the clumps of weeds as handholds. Yank loose too easily and then . . . " He made a whooshing sound. "We're going slowly enough that you can't get lost and you won't fall. But if you should start to roll off the mountain, we don't want you pulling someone else down with you, *nu*? *You*, we can get by without, but we really need those supplies!"

Paris had not exaggerated the labor or the danger of the climb. Jack was impressed that the young man swarmed up and down the file of packmen, encouraging, praising, and cheering them on. "That's it! Just another hundred yards to the top. Keep going! It's all downhill after this."

Another hour passed, and they still had not reached the summit.

Coming back down the caravan line, Paris crawled

along beside the tall, gaunt man Jack had classified as an undertaker. The exhausted figure seemed plastered to the hillside. "See that clump of flowers?" Paris inquired. "That is one bunch of brush it's safe to use as a handhold. Deep roots in these Judean hills, eh?"

Jack also spoke the words, but it was the undertaker who gave them voice in 1948, "What are they called?"

"The Blood of the Maccabees," Paris replied. "Keep going! We're almost there."

And this time, it was the truth. Beyond the top of the slope was a plateau . . . and a row of carts and buses and taxicabs and jeeps waiting to carry the vital supplies to Jerusalem.

"You will be going back now," Paris instructed his crew. "I'm proud of you. Thank you. Hungry children in Jerusalem thank you. *HaShem* thanks you."

"Aren't you coming back with us?" one of the waiters asked.

"No, I'm needed in Jerusalem," Paris returned. "When I'm not carrying rice and flour, I know how to handle explosives."

"At least tell us your name," the undertaker suggested. "So we can find you again, after, you know . . . "

"Why not?" Paris mused. "After tonight, we are brothers in arms, eh? My name is Sol . . . Sol Baruch. And now, Shalom!"

"Jack. Jack?" Bette's voice seemed to come from very

far away. "Are you all right?"

The amber sun dipped its toe in the Mediterranean. A dozen laughing surfers shrieked their pleasure at successfully mastering the small waves.

"Yes, I'm . . . fine," Jack returned. "And I have quite a story to tell you. Now. Right now, before I forget any of it."

12

The big bouquet was the last thing Jack bought in the Mahane Yehuda Market. One more item to carry was almost a bridge too far. Both arms overflowing, he made his way through the bustling Old City Jerusalem lanes to Bette's flat.

High, stone walls, pierced by an ornate iron gate, surrounded the two-story apartment building which was tucked away in a pedestrian lane near Christ Church. Juggling bags of bread and fresh fruit and at least two of every variety of edible thing he knew she liked, Jack used his elbow to ring the entrance buzzer. A metal mezuzah hung on the left pillar.

Bette's cheerful Israeli accent greeted him over the

speaker, "What's all this?"

He grinned sheepishly around the flowers into the security camera. "I came by way of the *souk.*"

"Crazy American tourist," she laughed. "A girl can never have too many flowers." The bolt clicked and allowed entry into a cool garden where a carved stone fountain was surrounded by exuberant blooms identical to those in Jack's bouquet.

A mosaic table with two wrought-iron chairs and a striped blue umbrella was set for lunch beside the water. Jack paused a moment to take in Bette's world.

She emerged from the building carrying a tray of sandwiches and a bottle of chilled white wine. Her face was still too thin, and her pace was still too slow, even after long weeks of specialized physical therapy in Tel Aviv.

"Welcome home."

"Jack! What have you done?"

"I couldn't come without a homecoming gift. Groceries. From the *souk.*"

She set the tray on the table and gave him a peck on the cheek. "If you're going to shop like an Israeli you must have a shopping trolley. You know, the bag with the wheels so you can fill it up and pull it along after." Taking the bouquet, she pretended to be impressed. "Thank you, my friend."

He didn't like it that she called him *friend.* Not after all they had been through together. "So maybe it *is* possible for a girl to have too many flowers?"

"Never. These will be for my kitchen table. Perfect. Come on then, bring your groceries inside. It isn't much, but it is home."

He followed her into the foyer. The Jerusalem stone floor was worn but ageless. Jack guessed this was one of the ancient buildings occupied by Old City Jews before their expulsion in 1948. Many structures had been rebuilt following the 1967 war, when the Old City was recaptured by the Israelis after nineteen years of Jordanian occupation. Eight mailboxes with combination locks set into the wall were vintage. Bette's flat was the first door on the left in the ground floor corridor.

She smiled over her shoulder. "I was so afraid I would have to give this place up. Stairs, you know. So steep. It's tiny, but I love it." She remained in the hall as he entered. "Put the bags on the table."

The living space was open to a small kitchen with a 1950's range, a pale green retro refrigerator, and a microwave. An old wooden table was splashed with layers of turquoise, red, and yellow paint, and flanked by four unmatched chairs. Two stainless steel kitty bowls sat empty on the floor by the sink. The cat was nowhere to be seen.

He set the groceries down but lingered.

The walls of the living area were awash with the colors of the Chagall blue angel poster and illuminated by two tall, arched windows protected by iron grates. A white iron daybed beneath the windows was covered by a woven quilt with as many colors as Joseph's coat, and at least a dozen pillows. An entire wall of shelves was cluttered with books and mementos and family photographs. He was sure that everything meant something in her life. No time to study them, though he wanted to. A small, flat-screen television opposite was Bette's only nod to letting the modern world inside. To the right, a steep, narrow stairway led to the upstairs bedroom. Mysterious. Private. For her eyes only. What was it like, Jack wondered?

"Come on," she said impatiently. "Lunch is in the garden."

"Just drinking you in."

"Wine is in the garden for drinking in."

His eyes swept over the room. He imagined her stretched out on the daybed with the cat curled up beside her as she read Hemingway or Steinbeck or Agatha Christie or P. G. Wodehouse.

Parked beside the door was her blue plaid shopping trolley, with wheels and a handle. "Next time, can I borrow this?" he asked.

"Sorry. You'll have to get your own. This belonged to my Sephardic grandmother. It rolled along at her heels like an obedient little dog."

Jack followed her outside. "But I'm a guest in your country . . . "

"It's infused with years of her bargaining prowess. The

vendors heard those wheels coming and trembled. I feel powerful when I take it with me to the market."

"Hmph." Jack mumbled. "Good to be home?"

"I didn't know if I would ever be back." Bette inclined her head toward an orange tabby cat, the color of cantaloupe, lounged in the shade of a jacaranda tree. "A million stray cats in Jerusalem. No one really owns them. But this one? When I got home, I can't tell you how happy I was to see him. *My* stray cat, you know?"

"Someone must have fed him. Biggest cat I've ever seen."

"I made it a habit over the years to never name a cat that hangs around. The minute I name them, they disappear. But when this guy started coming around a couple years ago, I named him."

"Should I ask?"

"You'll laugh."

"Try me."

"Jack. I named him Jack."

"Prophetic." Jack laughed.

"Well, he's still here, anyway. After everything. He didn't wander off."

"Two Jacks could get confusing. You'll have to rename one of your strays."

"I've thought of it. 'Me-lohn,' I think."

Jack repeated the word and speculated, "What's that? My lion?"

"Nothing so classy. Me-lohn. Melon. Cantaloupe. His color, you know?"

"If you called me a melon I might not stick around. Lion, I think. Lion is better."

"Okay, then. You will be Jack and Jack will be, 'Lavi.'" She tossed the feline a piece of roasted chicken. "How do you like it? The American thinks you look like a *lavi.*" The cat battled the morsel with his paw and blinked lazily at the couple.

Jack crossed his arms and narrowed his eyes. "He didn't go hungry."

"I promise, he pretends to belong to several other families in the neighborhood, but he belongs to no one. And I don't mind pretending he's mine."

Jack wondered, was she talking about Jack the cat or Jack the man?

"Your ability to speak in double entendre has not strayed, either."

"I confess I had to relearn small talk in rehab. But not everything I have to say is as easy as renaming a cat."

Endless days and weeks of physical rehab after the attack had brought Bette back from the edge of oblivion. Thankfully, she had been in peak physical condition, or she would not have survived. "But they have told me they don't think I will be able to return to duty."

Jack was relieved; happy with the news, but he did not tell her so. "I know what it meant to you."

"So, I ask myself, what do I do? What should I do now, Jack? My whole life was *Yamam*, you know? Anti-terror task force. My purpose. Especially now, with what is happening in Jerusalem." She sipped her wine and looked past him as though she was trying to see into her future.

"Like we spoke with Lev and Katy about: so many prophecies are coming to pass in Israel now. Ancient things are being revealed."

She nodded and pursed her lips together. "And that is what I wanted to talk to *you* about. To tell you. Ask you, really. Something happened. Something I can't explain. I couldn't tell anyone else. No one in all the world. I have something I need to ask you, and I'm only just now ready."

Jack leaned forward. "Of course, Bette."

"Okay, then. I don't even know . . . where do I start?"

"Wherever you can."

"I will just ask you then," she whispered. "Jack? Something happened. It was a night you were there, at the hospital."

He leaned back in his seat and inhaled deeply. "You know there were days when we weren't sure if you would live."

"No. More than just that. I mean . . . how do I explain this? An event. Something in ICU. I don't know what day. What time of day. But I think it was night. The doctors had just finished surgery. You were there. Am I right?"

Jack nodded, remembering the moment he thought she

was gone. "Yes. There was one night in ICU, right around 3:00 a.m. You were on life support. I had just dozed off and . . . "

Bette completed his sentence. "The deep of night. I saw myself. Very pale."

"Pale. Yes. The color of the wall."

"And I saw you standing over me. Beside the bed. Holding my hand. You were praying, I think I was hovering above you. An alarm went off, and suddenly there were people all around me. Doctors and nurses. You stood back against the wall and watched. I heard you say over and over, 'Bette, please don't go,' pleading like a little boy."

"How could you know this?"

"It did happen that way, didn't it?"

Jack swallowed hard, remembering the critical night when her heart stopped beating. The doctors swarmed in to try to revive her. "Yes. Just like that."

Bette frowned, "There's more. Jack, there were things I saw. Things you didn't see."

"Tell me. Please."

She paused. Sunlight fell on her hair and shoulders as she relived the moment. She shook her head. "I can't. I can't. Not just now. Maybe someday when I figure it out. But I can't explain. Jack, I am here now, not knowing why, except that I didn't want to leave you."

"I'm glad you didn't, Bette."

"You said my name again and again. And Jack, the

thing is, I am alive in this world, and suddenly I realize all the things I don't know. All the things I need to learn and need to know. But I don't know where to begin. It was a good start with Lev and Katy! But oh, Jack, I am hoping you will help show me."

"Funny thing. I feel the same way. So much I don't know. Too much to learn in a lifetime, I think. But maybe we can learn it together."

"Then, I will know what my purpose is. To go on this journey and finally reach the end and have all the answers? That is what I hope for."

13

Westering sunlight cradled the stones of Jerusalem in a golden embrace. Jack and Bette, Katy and Lev, and Dodi relaxed on the sofas of the Mamilla Hotel's rooftop restaurant. At eye level with the Temple Mount, their menus remained untouched as they drank in the panorama of three thousand years of the Holy City.

"It's not possible to explain the effect of this place to someone who hasn't been here," Jack said, breaking the reverie.

"There is nowhere else on earth like it," Dodi agreed. It's not just because of centuries and centuries of history. Lots of places can claim that quality. But here. Here . . . " She paused, lost in thought. "This is the epicenter of God's interaction with humans. The whole world is His. He created it. But prophets, priests, kings, scholars, warriors, and the Son of God Himself unite in declaring the significance of Jerusalem."

Jack likewise elaborated, "Everywhere you look demands that you look longer, dig deeper . . . except right here, of course. *Don't* look at these lime-green cushions." He plucked at the neon-bright fabric. Bette dug her elbow into his ribs from one side, and Dodi repeated the action from the other. Both women tried to shush him. "I mean," he continued over their correction, "who thought lime green was a good idea?"

"Time to stop, dear," Dodi added. "Just because you have a touch of Jerusalem syndrome doesn't mean you should cover your nervousness with forced humor."

Embarrassed, Jack lowered his chin until Dodi continued, "Besides, the cushions are 'chartreuse.'"

Her tablemates, including Jack, exploded with laughter. "Never argue color synonyms with an artist," Dodi concluded.

Redirecting the conversation, Bette offered, "Something I can never get over is how close together everything is here. For instance, how far do you think it is from here to the Dome of the Rock?"

Jack and Lev each shaded their eyes with upraised hands like wilderness scouts. The two men exchanged a glance, then nodded. "A couple miles," Lev said.

"Mile and a half," Jack suggested.

Turning to Dodi, Bette asked, "I bet you know, don't you?"

"Of course, dear," Dodi agreed. "It's only a kilometer, less than three-quarters of a mile. My boys, Sol and his friends, fought over this ground in '48 and again in '67, so I have good reason to know every meter."

When the waiter approached, Bette suggested a bottle of the Yarden Sauvignon Blanc from the Golan Heights winery.

The discussion continued. "Do you think the site of the Temple is directly under the Dome of the Rock?" Jack asked Lev.

"I do," Lev agreed. "And so do a number of historians and archaeologists. But there are other, equally respected scholars who say the Foundation Stone is not the outcropping under the Dome. They think it is actually buried under the pavement somewhere between the Dome and the al-Aqsa mosque."

"Foundation stone? Meaning, the place where Abraham was prevented from sacrificing Isaac?"

"True, but also the location of the threshing floor," Dodi added.

Lev nodded.

"Okay, wait," Jack protested. "What's this about a threshing floor?"

Using both hands to suggest a broad, flat area, Lev

figuratively brushed all the existing structures off the Temple Mount. "King David purchased a threshing floor from Araunah the Jebusite. Up there. The king wanted to build the Temple there. He wasn't allowed to, but Solomon used that same location when it was the right time."

"Because it was the highest point around, and because it was already a flat rock sturdy enough to hold up the foundations?"

"No . . . " Lev drawled in his curious 'Israel-by-way-of-Texas' accent. "The answer's more complicated than that."

"King David got himself in trouble with the Almighty," Dodi suggested. "Even though the Lord told him not to do so, the king took a census of the people."

"What's wrong with that?"

"It was wrong because David wanted to know how powerful an army he could lead into battle, instead of just trusting the Lord to win the battles no matter the odds."

Jack narrowed his eyes. "A male ego thing. Good to know I never have that problem."

Bette punched him playfully in the bicep.

"Ouch! Okay, okay. So David messed up. Then what?"

"The Almighty gave him a choice," Dodi continued. "Years of famine, months of being chased by enemy soldiers, or three days of a terrible plague."

A mix of unhappy cries reached Jack's hearing. They sounded like pain, grief, and terror all mingled together. "Do you hear that?" he asked, looking around the table . . .

at friends who were no longer seated there. Gone, too, were the lime-green cushions and the furniture. The entire rooftop restaurant was gone.

Instead, Jack followed a procession of bearded men in robes trudging through dusty, deserted streets. As Jack watched a dead body was dragged from a house where the people wept and sobbed. The corpse was tossed onto a cart already piled high with the dead.

One man, taller than the others, and more regal in form despite the sackcloth he wore, looked on. Ashes marred his tangled hair and wiry beard. The noble remarked, "What is the death toll?"

"My king, it is seventy thousand."

"So many? So many?" King David mourned. "Wasn't it I who commanded the people to be numbered? I am the one who sinned, but these people, my sheep, what have *they* done?"

The hike through the tragedy led upwards to the plateau where the Temple would one day exist. On a stone platform at the highest elevation, a team of servants was threshing wheat under the watchful eye of a foreman. One man led a yoke of oxen around in slow circles to loosen the grain from the stalks. Another man used a flail to knock the kernels of wheat free of the heads. Another pair of men wielding wooden pitchforks worked over a similar heap of grain and debris piled nearby. As they tossed each forkful aloft, the breeze over the mountaintop blew away the chaff while the clean grain fell back to earth.

Suddenly, there appeared an apparition, three times the height of a man, hovering in the air between heaven and earth. It was an angel with a drawn sword.

The entire king's retinue, including Jack, fell on their faces. So did the workers threshing the grain, but not their supervisor, who turned from observing the angel to studying the king.

Jack heard the prostrate king repeat his mournful confession and prayer.

A figure Jack had come to recognize as a prophet approached the king. "Hear what the Lord says, O King. '*I have restrained the angel, here by the threshing floor of Araunah. It is enough.*'"

The destroying angel remained poised with his sword held over Jerusalem. Hesitantly, fearfully, David and his men stood and dusted themselves off.

The supervisor of the threshing floor approached the king and bowed. "So, Araunah," David said. "Grant me this threshing floor that I may build an altar to the Lord here. Grant it to me at the full price so the plague will be halted from the people."

Araunah replied, "But I give it to you, O King! Also, take the wooden tools and the yoke to kindle the fire on the altar, and take the oxen for the sacrifice."

King David shook his head in vehement disagreement. "I will not take what is yours for the Lord. I will not make a burnt offering that costs me nothing." David directed the counting out of the full price for the land, the tools, the oxen, and the heaps of grain.

As Jack watched, an altar was constructed there on the threshing floor of Araunah. And when the sacrifice was prepared, fire fell from heaven and ignited the offering. Then the angel disappeared, and so did the scene from before Jack's eyes.

"Shall we order another bottle of wine, Jack? Jack?"

"Threshing out sin and disobedience and impurity . . . I get it," Jack said. "And, I won't make an offering that costs me nothing."

"Sorry, what?" Bette asked. "Jack, are you alright?"

Nodding knowingly Dodi suggested, "A touch of Jerusalem syndrome, dear?"

✡ ✡ ✡

With the Jericho 941 pistol beside his pillow, Jack slept soundly. Somewhere far away, a dog barked. Jack stirred and inhaled the scent of Dodi's night-blooming jasmine.

He was suddenly aware of Eliyahu's presence in the room.

"Jack?"

"I'm awake." Jack opened his eyes and sat up. "Since I saw King David and the threshing floor, I've been expecting another visit from you."

Across the Old City rooftops, faint moonlight glowed on the Temple Mount. Eliyahu, his silhouette framed against the shimmer of countless stars, stood in front of the window.

"You prayed for wisdom."

"I prayed you would come. There are so many things I don't understand. I felt it especially today. I don't even know what I don't know . . . what questions to ask?"

"For those who ask with a desire for Holy Wisdom, the Father pours it out with joy. The name of this prayer in Hebrew is called, *kavanah:* the prayer of deep and sincere longing; a prayer of the heart's intent. *Kavanah* is always heard in heaven and answered."

Eliyahu raised his arms like the conductor of an orchestra. As he moved his hands, sparks of light and color began to swirl around him. He moved his finger from right to left, and the Hebrew letters, *Kaf, Vav, Nun,* and *Heh,* blazed in the air and hung there.

"Kavanah." Jack thought that it was something like when a child with a sparkler spells his own name in the air, only the letters did not vanish.

"You surely recognize the sound of the word," Eliyahu smiled, and the light around him grew brighter.

"Yes!" Jack laughed. "The name of the new American Supreme Court Justice!"

"Everything means something." Eliyahu seemed pleased. "Why was he opposed? Why slandered? Why cursed by witches?"

"Kavanaugh opposes abortion."

"Child sacrifice. The worship of Ba'al by the sacrifice of infants caused the destruction of Israel. And this abomination will also bring great and terrible judgment on Israel's greatest ally, America."

Suddenly dots began to connect in Jack's mind. "The United States has recognized Jerusalem as the undivided capital of Israel."

"And the prince of this world is furious. For he knows all things . . . all the pieces of the prophetic puzzle . . . are falling into place."

Jack sat up and put his feet on the floor. The floor was cold. This was no dream. "What have I forgotten to ask?"

"As the Lord of Heaven uses men to fight for His kingdom, so does Satan use men. So Jack, do you know the name of the man who funded the opposition to Kavanaugh, and to your President, and who seeks to destroy your country? Who is he who funds the political chaos in your country, and throughout the world? Who is the Jew who spent a lifetime hating Israel?"

Once again, Eliyahu swept his hand through the air, this time spelling a Greek word; "*Sigma, omicron, rho, omicron, sigma.*"

As the Greek letters burned beside the Hebrew letters for Kavanah, Jack searched his memory for ancient, biblical Greek. Beginning and ending with the letter 's,' the letters formed a palindrome; the same word when read backwards or forwards. In Greek it meant a funeral bier, the stretcher for carrying dead bodies to the grave . . . a funeral urn for the keeping of human bones.

"Soros," Jack whispered in awe, finally understanding. "He's all about death."

"Yes." Eliyahu swept the name away with a stroke of his hand. "And there is so much more to tell than this. All connected. Light versus Darkness. Life and Death. Threshing out the grain . . . and falling on your face to pray for deliverance from evil."

"I want to know," Jack pleaded. "I need to know, you see?"

"Letter by letter, all will be revealed when the time is right. For now, there is too much for you to grasp."

Jack was suddenly exhausted. He put his hands to his face, and when he lowered them again, Eliyahu had vanished.

14

The courtyard of Dodi's house was alive with the scents of jasmine and sweet peas, and with music. Dodi, Bette, Jack, and a smiling Lev sat in rapt attention as Katy played her fiddle.

Nobody would accuse me of being a musician, Jack thought. *But I know this piece. Debbie and I heard it performed at Westminster Cathedral. Psalm 136, but the composer used some Sephardic phrases. I wish I had paid closer attention to the meaning.*

Streamers of clouds stretched across the oblong of sky visible over Dodi's terrace. While Jack watched, the banners of vapor coalesced into a solid wall that advanced from west to east over the city. Not only did the cloud thicken dramatically, it also sunk toward the ground until the lowest tendrils of mist curled about the tree branches.

Jack stared upward, losing himself in the music and in memories of Debbie that left him confused and oddly guilty feeling. The fog drifted lower still until it was difficult to see Bette across the patio from him.

He was not surprised to find himself standing . . . somewhere . . . different. Nor was he alarmed to notice Eliyahu standing beside him. Vapor continued to surround them, but its source was no longer clouds overhead. The mist was flooding from the entrance to a grand building that loomed just ahead: thirty feet wide and monstrously tall, the upper reaches were swallowed by the cloud.

"Today is the dedication of the Temple built by King Solomon," Eliyahu explained. "It was constructed over Araunah's threshing floor that King David purchased. Now the flat space where the plague was stopped and the people spared is directly beneath the Holy of Holies, inside the inner veil. Over it is the Ark of the Covenant and the outstretched wings of the cherubim."

An enormous altar stood outside the entry to the Temple. At the side opposite to the sanctuary entrance were hundreds of musicians dressed in white. While one hundred twenty trumpeters punctuated the hymn, the harps, the lyres, the cymbals, and the vocalists combined as one great hymn of praise:

Give thanks to the Lord, for He is Good. For His mercy endures forever!

Psalm 136, like in Katy's music.

"Once the holy Ark of the Covenant was installed in the Temple," Eliyahu explained, "the sacrifices began. What you see pouring out of the sanctuary is not smoke. It is the visible presence of the Almighty . . . the *Shekinah* glory . . . expressing His approval of the worship, especially the music."

Jack became aware that besides the priests and the musicians and the other Levite attendants at the House of God, the plaza of the Temple was filled with thousands of worshippers.

The music reached a triumphant climax, then stopped.

A royal figure, resembling King David, but taller, more fair in coloring, and less broad in the shoulders, mounted a bronze platform where he could be seen by all.

The king knelt down, then lifted his hands toward heaven and said, *"Lord God of Israel, there is no God in heaven or on earth like You, who keeps Your covenant and mercy with Your servants who walk before You with all their hearts."*

As Solomon continued, the king put God in remembrance of previous promises: that Solomon's father, David, would be the first of a continuous line of kings of Israel, if God's people always walked in His ways.

Then the king sketched out the terms of an agreement between the Almighty and His People. God would always listen to prayers made toward the Temple . . . that He would hear from heaven and forgive their sins . . . that He would provide relief from the issues of drought and of plague . . . that He would guide and strengthen them in battle.

"And when they are carried captive to a land far or near, and there repent and make supplication and return to You with all their heart and all their soul, and offer their prayers toward this place, You will forgive them and maintain their cause."

Jack was struck by the prophetic words of the king. The descendants of these worshippers . . . *Me!* Jack thought . . . would be carried away from the land as captives, and dispersed around the world as exiles, but they would never stop praying for their return here.

When the threshing was complete, and the disobedience purged . . . when the purified wheat was gathered from the chaff . . . it would be at this spot in the whole universe that the longing would be fulfilled.

"Now, therefore," Solomon concluded, *"Arise, O Lord God, to Your resting place, You and the Ark of Your strength. Let Your priests, O Lord God, be clothed with salvation, and let Your saints rejoice in goodness. O Lord God, do not turn away the face of Your Anointed; remember the mercies of Your servant David."*

Solomon was invoking the coming of the Messiah! Jack realized, a thousand years before Jesus was born.

Enthusiastic expressions of awestruck wonder erupted from thousands of mouths as fire fell from heaven and ignited the wood of the sacrifice on the altar. The entire company of onlookers, including Jack and Eliyahu, fell on their faces, chanting, *"Give thanks to the Lord, for He is good.*

His Mercy endures forever."

When the holy scene dissolved along with the mist, Jack was once again in the midst of those he loved and who loved him . . . home, in Jerusalem.

—————————————   ✡ ✡ ✡   —————————————

After Lev and Katy had taken their leave, Bette and Dodi sat quietly enjoying their tea in the pleasant air of Dodi's courtyard. Jack, meanwhile, paced up and down like a caged tiger.

Bette studied him with concern. Dodi caught the young woman's eye, made a calming gesture with her hands, and whispered, "He's putting together a question. You'll see. His grandfather was the same way, but it'll come out soon."

The edges of the terrace were ringed with potted plants, some of which Jack recognized, like mint and dill, but others were unknown. He glanced an inquiry at Dodi. "My herb garden," she said. "I'm trying to grow one of every herb or spice mentioned in scripture."

Jack nodded without replying and continued pacing.

The potted plants punctuated a margin of fruit trees. There was citrus with dark green, shiny leaves, and fragrant white blossoms. Another tree glistened with a new crop of broad, pale leaves that resembled the fingers of outstretched hands.

Jack stopped prowling and plopped down in a chair

beside Bette. "I have some questions for you," he said to his grandmother.

Raising one eyebrow slightly in Bette's direction, Dodi murmured, "Of course you do, dear. Go right ahead."

"I understand how God made a permanent commitment to His people . . . our people . . . about this land," he said. "After being dispersed throughout all the world, I get what a miracle it is for Israel to again exist. But my question is this: what's so urgent about right now? I mean, after seventy years why can't Israel just exist alongside its neighbors? And what does all this have to do with what's coming? And for that matter, what *is* coming?"

Setting her cup down Dodi remarked, "The way you phrase that query sounds a lot like the way Yeshua's disciples asked Him to teach them about the end of the world: 'When will these things be?' they asked, and 'What will be the sign of your coming?' and 'What will be the sign of the end of the age?' Remember, he had just shocked them."

"What do you mean?" Bette asked.

"His friends were admiring the Temple. The reconstruction and expansion had been going on for forty-some years, and it was one of the wonders of the world. But Yeshua told them all the stones they saw there would be thrown down."

"And He was talking about when the Romans destroyed the Temple in 70 A.D.," Jack offered. "I saw that happen

. . . in a vision, I mean."

Dodi continued, "So his friends thought if something that terrifying could happen to something so grand . . . so permanent-seeming . . . it must be right before the end of all things, right? Of course, right. But not so. Yeshua said there'd be wars, and famines, and plagues, and persecution, and lawlessness, and false prophets."

"But all of those things have happened over and over again for the last two thousand years," Jack complained. "When's it get . . . what am I trying to say? When does it get . . . final?"

"Ah!" Dodi exclaimed. "Impatient, just like them?" Pausing for thought, Dodi glanced around the terrace before continuing. Waving toward the tree whose leaves suggested fingers, she asked, "Do you know what sort of tree that is?"

Jack nodded. "Fig tree, right?"

"Yes. Well, in that same discussion, Yeshua told his friends they should take a lesson from the fig tree. He said that when it puts forth leaves, you know summer is near."

"Too cryptic for me," Jack complained.

"Every year my tree loses all its leaves," Dodi explained. "It even looks dead. But then, every Spring, it shows that the season of regrowth has come again. I suspect Bette knows what I'm speaking of."

Bette wrinkled her forehead. "Not really," she admitted. "Except . . . except my father always said Israel is like a fig tree. Is that part of it?"

"Bravo," Dodi praised. "The Prophet Hosea, speaking with the voice of the Almighty, says to Israel, 'I saw your fathers as the first fruits on the fig tree in its first season." Turning toward Jack and lifting her chin, Dodi challenged, "Can you put it together now?"

"The question was about the end of the world or about the return of the Messiah," Jack mused aloud. "Yeshua had just said that Jerusalem was going to experience a terrible disaster, including the great diaspora . . . Jews driven out of the land and scattered throughout the world. So . . . "

Dodi was already nodding even before Jack resumed sharing his thoughts. "So . . . if the fig tree is putting out new leaves . . . after looking dead . . . and the tree is Israel . . . then the rebirth of Israel was a powerfully important . . . what? Sign? Signal?"

Nodding more vigorously than ever Dodi agreed. "This is the seventieth anniversary of the rebirth of the state. No nation has ever gone out of existence for anything like two thousand years and then been reborn."

Slowly, choosing his words carefully, Jack asked, "Don't you think that it was so unexpected for there to be an Israel again, that now . . . after the fact . . . people just try to find prophetic significance in the circumstance?"

"Do you know who Alfred Edersheim was?" Dodi posed.

Jack shook his head, so Dodi looked the question at

Bette, who also shrugged.

"A Jewish believer in Yeshua who lived in the mid-to-late 1800s. A historian. He wrote *The Life and Times of Jesus the Messiah*, among other things. Edersheim suggested that the most important event of two millennia would be the return of the Jews to the land of Israel, and the rebirth of the nation. And . . . he made these statements fifty years before Israel again existed."

Jack made no reply, and Dodi raised her chin. "You know how long I have lived here now, eh? Long enough that almost a whole generation has passed since those miraculous events! And what else did Yeshua say, at the same time He spoke of the fig tree? He said, 'The generation that sees all these things happen—'the fig tree'—the nation restored—'will not pass away until all these things take place.'"

Bette lowered her eyes. She had been unconsciously twisting and untwisting her napkin, and she stopped abruptly.

Jack offered a one-syllable comment, "Wow."

"Wow, indeed," Dodi concurred.

Glancing at Bette, Jack said, "I think that's more than enough to chew on for one day."

Dodi agreed. "Just one more thing, though," she added. "In that same discussion . . . talking about when He would return . . . Yeshua gave one more sign that can't be fulfilled yet. He talked about the abomination of desolation standing in the Holy Place."

"Like Antiochus did in the days of the Maccabees," Jack noted. "And also what happened when the Romans destroyed the Temple and defiled the mount again?"

Tilting her head slightly, Dodi remarked. "But for the abomination to stand in the Holy Place . . . "

Jack sat bolt upright. "There has to be a Temple. If that prophecy has an end-times fulfillment, there has to once again be a Temple for a false prophet . . . a false Christ . . . to defile!"

15

Jack was out of town, working with Lev and a group of American pastors. Bette, at first shy about asking, nevertheless asked Dodi if she could visit the artist again. "I don't want to impose . . . "

The warmth of the response reassured her. "Impose? Don't we both share love for a little boy who is trying to find his way? As I see it, my dear, we are allies! Perhaps even co-conspirators."

Dodi arranged a bouquet of flowers as Bette finished setting the table for their lunch.

"It's plain to see you are an artist," Bette laughed. "I just buy the flowers in the market and shove them into a vase. You make every bloom just so."

Dodi crossed her arms and studied her creation. "From my days studying art at the Sorbonne. Every bloom in every bouquet we set in place as if it was a still-life painting. The reds in this dominate all the other blooms. You know the name of this flower?"

"*Dam ha Makabim*. Blood of the Maccabees. For Israel's Memorial Day. I know the legend that in every spot the flower grows, a drop of blood has been spilled on this earth."

"In Arabic it is called *dam al-Massiah*, meaning Blood of Christ. Red flowers for remembrance. For beauty, for color and light. I think one could sit for hours and gaze upon these and praise God."

Bette's smile faded. She frowned as she glanced at the bouquet and then looked away. "Beautiful, but . . . "

"What is it, child?"

"Red. The color of our wounds. So much suffering. So many fallen. And the innocent who died just because they are Jews."

"Red Everlasting. We will not forget."

"Dodi, there is something else. Something I saw. I have not told anyone."

"Yes?"

"I don't know where to begin. Red Everlasting. These flowers. Blooming wild everywhere on the hillsides of Israel. Dodi, I don't know how to begin. I wanted to tell Jack, but I can't think how to explain this. What I saw. It sounds so crazy. It makes no sense, really."

"I will be happy to listen if you would like to tell me. Without judgment."

Bette sat across from Dodi. The old woman's gentle smile and kind eyes coaxed Bette to share her secret. Gnarled hands served the meal.

"It was when I was in the hospital. ICU. Late at night. It happened in the beginning, when they weren't sure if I would live. I was on life support. Jack was there in the room. I saw him. But I didn't see him with my eyes. Not as I see you now . . . "

Food remained untouched on their plates as Bette's story tumbled out.

Dodi encouraged her with a solemn nod. "Yes. I understand."

"And I saw myself. I saw myself, frail and white, in the hospital bed . . . with a breathing tube down my throat and wires and IVs and bags of fluids hanging from metal racks. There was a monitor behind me. The heartbeat graph moving across the screen. I thought how much it looked like the silhouette of mountain peaks. Then there were blood pressure numbers. Well, all of it. I saw it all, you see. But I couldn't have seen it with my eyes because my eyes were closed and I was just . . . gazing down on my body and watching as suddenly all the lines on the graph all went flat. Alarms went off, and Jack sprang up. The room filled with people. Nurses and doctors working over me. Giving orders. I tried to tell them I was right there, but they didn't hear me. Jack was standing in the corner out of the way. He was talking to me and begging, 'Don't leave me, Bette. I can't survive if you leave me.' Then he was praying. Just praying and begging God. Asking for my life to be given back."

Bette fell silent for a long moment. She raised her eyes to search Dodi's face. Did the old woman understand what Bette was telling her?

Dodi replied, "Yes. Jack called me the night of the crisis. He was weeping. Asked me to pray. Go on, please, my dear."

Bette exhaled slowly. "I died, you see. But not me, I mean I knew my body had died in that instant. I was in the room above it all. I witnessed it all."

"I believe you."

"That's not all. That's just the beginning of what happened."

Dodi leaned closer. "Take your time . . . "

"Well, then, everything changed. There was a great light before me in the distance. Brighter than anything I can explain. A pure light. Purity. But I was so impure. So imperfect. And I saw a man with his arms stretched out, and he was covered in wounds. Deep horrible wounds. And the blood and the light radiated from his wounds. He looked straight at me with eyes so filled with sorrow and yet so compassionate and full of love for me. And I began to sob. I fell down in front of him, and his pierced hands were reaching toward me." Tears came to Bette's eyes and spilled down her cheeks. "Then I could see my name was carved on the palms of his hands. Blood red; the deep red color of these flowers of remembrance. Then I gasped because I could see clearly, in the letters of my name, there were *dam ha Makabim* blooms. The flowers grew in the blood of the wounds." Bette stared at the palms of her hands. "And I heard his voice . . . no. No, I *felt* his voice speak to me, '*dam al-Massiah.*' Blood of Christ."

Dodi said, "It is written, '*We will look upon him whom we have pierced.*'" Silence for an instant, then Dodi whispered, "By his wounds we are healed."

"I cry every time I think of it. The vision of my name and of his suffering still haunts me." Bette wiped away tears with her napkin. "And then? Then I was back. Back in my own body. Back in the hospital. In terrible pain. Struggling to breathe. All of the staff around me. Someone said, 'We've got a heartbeat.' And then? Then? I don't know what. I just knew I had to be here. I had to live for some reason, but I don't know what it all means. Dodi? Do you know?"

Dodi reached across the table and took Bette's hand. "Darling girl, there is something you must see; a place here in Jerusalem near New Gate and the Old City which you must visit. Notre Dame of Jerusalem, it's called. I promise when you see, it will explain much."

-------------------- ✿ ✿ ✿ --------------------

For reasons she could not explain, Bette had slipped away
from her shadowing bodyguard for this excursion. Despite
the increased danger, she needed to explore this mystery
alone. She had heard the name 'Notre Dame' in her hospital
vision and then again from Dodi. If 'everything means
something,' then this coincidence was a good place to begin.

Bette knew well the destination to which Dodi had
directed her.

She stepped off the bus at #3 Paratroopers Road, north
of the Old City. Before her loomed the imposing structure
of the Pontifical Institute: Notre Dame of Jerusalem. The
flowerbeds were thick with small red blooms.

Whose blood spilled in this soil, Bette mused? The
Maccabees? Or perhaps the blood of the Messiah?

Twin crenelated battlements that exuded the aura of
a medieval Crusader castle marked entry to the structure.
On the parapet between the towers stood a huge statue
of Mary with the infant Jesus carried joyfully on her left
shoulder.

Bette was aware that the Institute had provided rooms
for pilgrims for over one hundred years. It contained
several restaurants, as well as the Terra Sancta Museum.
Among displays of thousands of ancient artifacts excavat-

ed from Jerusalem, the museum also housed a permanent exhibit of the Shroud of Turin.

Bette considered how strange it was that she had lived within the shadow of the Institute for her entire life, but only now, encouraged by Dodi, was she crossing the threshold for thc first time.

"There is an exhibit here. The Crucified Man," she explained to the attendant.

"Free Admission," he replied. With a wave of his hand, he directed her toward the entry.

The room was dark and surprisingly no one else was there. Bette pushed open the door and lights came up. She gasped as her eyes fell on a familiar face and a recognizable wounded body; the same as in her vision. The life-size, bronze sculpture of a crucified man, his form covered in wounds from scourging and torture, lay in the midst of multiple display cabinets.

Bette was grateful no one else was in the room. She slowly approached the prone figure of the executed man and stood over him, gazing in horror at the wounds and vicious stripes that covered him.

Words she had heard in her vision came to her, *"By his wounds you are healed . . . "*

Tears streamed down her cheeks.

"You will look upon Him whom you have pierced and weep . . . "

"Yes," Bette answered quietly as teardrops fell on the

torn hands of the crucified man. "It was you I saw then. You! Yeshua. Salvation."

She recalled again her ICU vision in death of tiny red blooms sprouting where his blood had spilled.

"I'm so sorry. Such agony," she whispered. "I would have tried to save you from them, you know. If I had been there that morning on Via Dolorosa as you stumbled beneath their blows I would have fought them. If only I had been there."

Then the memory of his voice returned to her. As she hovered above her body in ICU, He had spoken her name, *"Bette, heart of a warrior. Yes. You would have fought to save me, but it was I who died for you."*

Died for her? What did He mean by those words?

Her shoulders shook in silent sobs. She remained alone, weeping over the body of the crucified man.

It was a long time before Bette turned away from the dead man who lay frozen in time on a cold, stone slab, in a hand-hewn tomb.

Raising her eyes at last, Bette took in the full-sized, exact replica of the Shroud of Turin, flanked by a life-sized Roman cross.

Crucifixion nails the length of railroad spikes had been driven through the victim's hands and feet. Wood-handled whips with lead-tipped leather strands had ripped his flesh. Muscle had been torn down to the bone with every lash. The gruesome torment of this Roman method of execution was described in detail.

And then there was a woven crown of thorns; a cap of spikes that had been shoved deep into his scalp.

"Behold the King of the Jews," the Roman soldiers had mocked.

Bette could hardly breathe.

King of the JEWS? Her King! The King of her people? Son of David! The monarch of all of Israel!

Studying the implements of Roman brutality, she grasped the reality of the death of the King of the Jews. Two thousand years ago in Jerusalem, Herod, the Jewish religious leaders, and the Roman governor had been threatened by the popularity and power of Jesus. If Jesus could heal the sick, feed five thousand from five loaves of bread and two fish, and give life back to the dead, could He not also raise an invincible army?

Yes. Jesus of Nazareth had to die, or all their secular power would have been lost.

She gazed at the Shroud. The image of a tortured, dead, Jewish King, front and back, was somehow imprinted on the surface of that ancient linen fabric. In an inexplicable burst of energy and light, something had happened to capture the grim image of the dead man encased within the Shroud.

Could it be that what the Christians believed about Jesus was true? Was this the image of the instant between death and resurrection?

Bette did not know how long she lingered in the room. At last an Italian-speaking tour group bumbled in and interrupted her quiet reverie.

She turned away, and left through the castle doors as the sun was setting. There were still so many unanswered questions.

Outside, beneath a King Lion palm tree, red blooms nodded on a slight breeze. *"Dam ha Makabim."*

She plucked a stalk and tucked it into her pocket.

Everything seemed changed as she took her seat on the green bus. Bette gazed out at the hewn stones of New Gate that opened into the cobbled lanes of the Old City and ultimately led to Via Dolorosa. Somehow, the distant past of Jerusalem was inextricably linked to the present and the future.

Touching the red flower she whispered, "Red Everlasting. Blood of Messiah."

——————————— ✿ ✿ ✿ ———————————

Bette caught the midnight #7 bus. Except for one black-clad Orthodox Jew in his early thirties, Bette was the only other passenger.

The Hassidic Jew sang off key as he listened to music through his earphones. Bette took a seat three rows behind the driver and pretended not to notice the bad karaoke rendition of Sonny and Cher's, "I Got You Babe."

CHAPTER 15

The eyes of the bus driver glanced at Bette in his rear view mirror and widened with amusement. "Russian," he explained to Bette. "With the new American Embassy opening in his neighborhood he's teaching himself to speak English by listening to American music."

Bette smiled as he drove on through the deserted streets of Jerusalem toward the Russian district of Arnona.

One more stop. The doors slid back and a bearded old man with a cane hobbled on board. A towering, skinny teenager with skin the color of black licorice followed. They were an unlikely pair, yet seemed to be traveling together. They exchanged conversation in a language Bette could not understand. Possibly Ethiopian?

The two sat opposite Bette. The black teen flashed Bette a pearl-toothed grin as the vehicle pulled away and the oblivious Hassid hit a particularly bad note. Bette smiled back and shrugged.

The old man remarked to the teenager in English, "So. Simeon? 'I Got You, Babe?' An oldie."

The black teen laughed. "Not so old as all that. Music brings people together, does it not, Elijah?"

"Depends."

The PA announced the arrival at the Diplomat Hotel where Russian immigrants had been housed by the Israeli government over the years. The 1960s style hotel had recently been purchased by the United States and would soon be part of the U.S. Embassy in Jerusalem.

The Russian Jew, singing the Abba song, "The Winner Takes It All," exited the bus.

"Back in five minutes." The driver stepped out and lit up a cigarette.

The old man and the teen remained seated and continued their conversation in fluent Hebrew as if Bette were invisible.

"Diplomat Hotel," said the old man. "The Americans will never know the significance of this place. It was on the border of divided Jerusalem. Jordan occupied East Jerusalem and Israel here in the west. Rooms overlooking No Man's Land and the Old City. You remember, Simeon?"

"As if it was yesterday," answered the teenager. "And then 1967 came when there was no more barbed wire and the landmines were taken out of the ground."

"But surely the greatest moment was during Shavuot, 1988. Pentecost."

The teenager threw his head back and laughed. "Yes. Yes. Here. Right here. The first sizable number of Jewish believers to gather in Jerusalem in two thousand years. Twelve hundred Jews who believed in Yeshua here in this hotel. And I was among them."

What? Bette stared at the boy.

Did they not know she spoke Hebrew? Startled by the young man's impossible declaration, she glanced away quickly lest they see she was listening. How could he claim to remember something that had happened before he was born?

The old man nodded. "Yes, Simeon.1988. It was. It is. It will be. Fulfillment. The return of Jews who recognize Yeshua their Messiah."

"Ah, how brightly the pillar of light shone down upon this place. It was declared that day, to them all, that one day Holy Fire would fill the building."

"And now America will have it as a part of their Embassy. Yes. Holy Fire will come, and a prophecy is fulfilled. What they will see in this American Embassy these days of Elijah is beyond their comprehension. But here is where it all began."

Bette stared down at her hands, afraid to look up at the two passengers. The bus lurched into motion again and slipped past the Diplomat Hotel, then onto the next stop.

Door banged open. Elijah and Simeon stood together and moved toward the exit. The old man paused directly in front of her and waited. Still Bette did not look up.

A long moment passed.

Elijah spoke softly. "Bette." He said her name. How did he know her name?

She turned her face up to look at him. Ancient eyes locked upon her. "Bette," he said again, but his mouth did not move.

"Yes," she replied.

He smiled, kindly. "Read Matthew, Chapter 24."

She nodded. "I will."

Then the two passengers left the bus.

Bette could not speak. Her breath was short. She turned to look back at the bus stop as the vehicle pulled away.

No one was there.

✡ ✡ ✡

Sleep eluded Bette. There was almost too much to think about to go to bed. She showered and put on her sweats, then mixed a batch of zucchini bread from her mother's recipe. The homey aroma filled her flat. Chamber music played softly. She crossed her arms and stared impatiently at the oven.

Carried on the scent of baking and the sweet sound of music, an old memory stirred: Bette could see herself, maybe seven or eight years old. Mama was slicing bread, then smiling over her shoulder in the kitchen, as Papa spread a handful of family treasures across the table.

Papa held up the small, round, fragment of stained glass, framed in a gold bezel. He had quietly admonished, "Never forget, Bette. Never forget who you are and where we come from . . . "

The timer rang, shattering her reverie. Bette took the steaming bread from the oven and set it to cool on the counter top. Then she retrieved a keepsake box from the top shelf of her closet.

This was the only thing she had taken from her family home after the massacre. She had never opened it . . . until now.

Placing it on the table, she inhaled deeply and lifted the lid. Family photos smiled up at her. Mother. Father. Brothers. Grandfather holding baby Benjamin. All of them.

Bette smiled back, longing.

Aching.

"I see you. Do you see me?" she whispered aloud. "What was it, Papa? What was it you told me to never forget?"

Beneath the photographs, a gleam of gold and cobalt blue caught her eye. She lifted the stack of photographs and Grandfather's leather-bound journal to reveal a heavy gold chain attached to a medallion. It was a round fragment of ancient stained glass, about the circumference of the palm of her hand. It was meant to be worn; almost like a badge of office.

"It was this, Papa," she said to his photo. "But why?"

Bette held it up so the light above the table shone through. Deep hues of blue and green and russet shone through the glass. A spiral scrap of something, rough and brown, seemed to be wrapped in a stem of brambles. It was a cherished fragment of some greater picture, but she could not understand its meaning or why her father had instructed her to never forget.

Opening her grandfather's journal, the unlined pages were crammed with archaic cursive German. It was not a language Bette had ever learned, nor did she ever wish to. But, was the answer to her questions within these pages?

She turned her attention to the medallion again. Stamped into the rim of the bezel in Hebrew were the words, "IF I FORGET THEE O JERUSALEM," and then the single word: "GOREN."

"Goren," Bette said quietly. "Threshing Floor." Turning the treasure over in her hands she studied the colors and the image.

Sudden exhaustion swept over her like a wave.

She replaced the treasures in the box and returned it to its place on the shelf. Maybe it did not mean anything.

Then she smiled as she switched off the light and remembered her grandfather saying, "Everything means something." *I need to show this to my friend*, she thought. *I need to show it to Jack.*

✧ ✧ ✧

After dinner, as Jack helped Bette clear the table and wash the dishes, she quietly recounted the story of her vision in the hospital and her visit to the Shroud exhibition.

As coffee brewed, she finished the tale with the story of angels on the bus, fresh baked zucchini bread and, at last, the mysterious medallion in the family keepsake box.

"Would you like to see it?" She was already rummaging in the closet.

"Very much." Jack was aware of what a step of trust this was for Bette to confide such a secret to him.

His breath caught and he felt a pang of emotion as the lid came off. The reality of the massacre of an entire Jewish family by Palestinian terrorists slammed home as Bette introduced him to her lost loved ones.

"Here. This is my mother and father." She passed Jack a photograph of a young couple holding a baby. Their chins were tucked and they squinted against the sun. "Yes. This is Papa holding me. I was very little here."

"Beautiful." Jack took the photograph reverently and studied it. "Your mother was beautiful. She looks a lot like you here." She plucked another from the sheaf. "This is my brother Benjamin when he was a baby. About the age I was in this one."

"Yes." Jack grinned. "I see the family resemblance."

She took it back from him, gazed at it tenderly, then closed her eyes and pressed it to her heart. "I think I did the right thing. You know? Adopted by the Silver family. A normal life for him. A family. A complete family to love him. Not just a sister; broken. Broken like me."

Jack put his hand on her arm and tried to protest, but it was no good. He understood the brokenness of terrible loss. "Bette . . . " he began.

She shook her head. "No. Broken. That's the right

word, Jack. You can't ever imagine the memory I carry." Her voice cracked. Silence fell across the little room for a long moment.

"Okay. Okay, you're right. No one can imagine. I'm sorry. They were such beautiful people."

"Happy. We were all happy. Even my grandfather. Even after everything he lived through in the Holocaust, Jack. I have to remind myself of that. Grandfather managed to have a life. A happy life even though . . . you know?"

"Yes. Remarkable. That's where you come from. It's who you are."

Bette gave a little laugh. "Funny you should say that. I mean at this very moment. Funny you say this is who I am. My father said I must never forget who I am or where I come from. And then he showed me this."

Bette extracted the stained glass medallion and held it up. The light and colors . . . azure and bronze and deep green . . . seemed to drip from her fingers. She passed it on to Jack.

He studied it for a moment, tracing the Hebrew letters along the rim of the golden bezel. "My Hebrew is passable, but I can't quite . . . "

She answered, "'If I forget thee O Jerusalem.' Then, 'Goren.' Threshing floor. I don't know what it means. I mean I can't figure out what the image is. Any guesses?"

"Colors are like the medieval stained glass in the great cathedrals of Europe; those that survived the war. Where does it come from?"

"My grandfather carried it away with him. I was too young to remember all the story when they told me, just that he managed to preserve it somehow. Hid it in a wall somewhere during the war and went back for it. But I don't know what it is. Or why it matters. Only that it meant something to him. And to my father. And it should mean something to me too."

Jack held it up to the light. There was something familiar about the dark spiral curve entwined by thorns. But what? "Bette, I know a guy at Oxford. An art historian. Specifically studies medieval stained glass. His whole life is restoration and preservation. I'd like to send him a few pictures. May I?"

"Yes!" she replied enthusiastically. 'Oh, yes!" She nudged the leather-bound journal toward Jack. "And this. Grandfather's journal. All in a sort of illegible German dialect. Do you know someone who might be able to help me translate?"

"Do you think the journal is connected to the medallion?"

"I don't know. They are Grandfather's. And they are together. So? Maybe?"

Jack mentally ran through his list of university professor friends. Yes, there were linguists among them. "Sure. Let me put it out there. We'll get some answers."

16

Dr. Simon Gross had been Jack's friend from his early
years at Oxford University. An expert on medieval art,
Simon had gone on to consult on and restore works of art
and stained glass in the cathedrals of Europe. It seemed
more than a coincidence to Jack that Simon had just taken
a sabbatical year to study at Hebrew University, and so was
nearby.

Simon held Bette's precious, stained-glass medallion
up to the light. The balding, bespectacled scholar squinted as he examined the artifact with a magnifying glass.
To Jack he thought aloud: "Of course. Of course. Clearly
medieval, yes. German, by its color palette. What's the
story?"

"Family tradition is that it was saved out of a destroyed synagogue; salvaged out of the holocaust. Nuremburg. We can't make out the significance of the image. If there is any? What is this? I can't imagine anyone going to such lengths to preserve a shard of glass unless it meant something."

"Personal memento, perhaps? Curious. Indeed. Not much medieval religious art is left from that area of Germany." He hummed softly. "Hebrew inscription. Interesting. On the bezel: the Hebrew word *Goren. Gimel, resh, nun.* Threshing floor. Within the glass itself, see here?" He pointed out tiny Hebrew letters on the edge of the image. "*Nun resh.* Which means, hmmm. *Neer.* The most descriptive would be . . . a newly plowed furrow. So you have the same Hebrew letters arranged in different words in the glass and on the bezel. One speaks of plowing; the violent breaking up of ground in a furrow to plant seeds. The other word, *Goren,* is the threshing floor; the time of harvest."

Jack nodded. "I understand the connection . . . but not the meaning."

Simon brushed past Jack's objection. "The answer is in the image of the medallion. Look here. There seem to be other Hebrew letters entwined within the thorns. But I am not certain . . . not certain enough to say definitively what it is."

"Any theories?"

CHAPTER 16

Simon shrugged. "Theories? Well, yes, Jack. Several. May I keep the medallion a few days? Do a little research before I venture an opinion?"

Jack agreed and left the treasure with Simon. He texted Bette on his way home to let her know that perhaps an answer was coming.

✡ ✡ ✡

It was late. The cat was asleep on the window ledge. Bette's cup of tea had long since grown cold.

A pool of light illuminated the yellowed sheet of paper that had been saved with the stained glass medallion.

Bette frowned at her grandfather's archaic handwriting.

His letter was dated November 29, 1947. . . the same date the United Nations voted to end British Mandatory rule and establish the homeland of Israel as refuge for the stateless Jewish people.

Spirals and elaborate swirls of ink were not easy to decipher.

Bette had been told as a child that Grandfather would never make use of the German language. In this letter to his wife, he wrote in English, the language of those who had liberated the survivors of the Nazi concentration camps.

"My dearest Deborah: On this very night it is decided by the nations that the Nation of Israel will arise. We are

thankful that we have lived to see this day! We heard the
vote on the wireless and prayed together, 'HEAR O Israel,
the Lord your G-d is One Lord.'

"My friend, Sol, said to us, 'Did not the Prophet Micah
write, *Zion will be plowed like a field; Jerusalem will become a heap
of rubble; the Temple hill a mound overgrown with thickets?* Have
they not plowed long furrows over our backs?'

"I answered, 'and yet it is written on my heart by the
finger of God that one day the Seed of Abraham will
again HEAR the threshing floor. He will gather the sheaves
of Israel in Jerusalem. Everything means something holy
for us now, my dear. Nothing is out of place. I believe,
as my father taught, that in our time, the Temple will be
rebuilt, and true priests of the ancient line will come forth
from hiding. In that time, as the prophets foretold, we will
see Messiah come to Yerushalayim.'"

Bette pressed her fingers to her forehead and puzzled
over her grandfather's strange wording. What did he
mean? 'Israel will HEAR the threshing floor?' Perhaps it
was Grandfather's unfamiliarity with the English language.

And yet, he had printed out the word, HEAR, in all
capital letters.

Bette carefully refolded the letter, slipped it back into its
envelope, and replaced it in the box of family mementos.
Perhaps Jack's friend would soon decipher the meaning of
the treasure.

PART III

17

Lev's unscheduled meeting with Jack took place in Lev's office at the Partners With Zion headquarters. "Netanyahu's office contacted me this morning," Lev said after catching Jack in the hallway. "Come in."

"What about?"

"They want to see you."

"Me? What for?" Jack was baffled at the unexpected request. Jack had been in Netanyahu's office exactly once, and on that occasion, he had been more an onlooker than a participant. "What's this about? Are they kicking me out of the country for stealing their prettiest girl?"

Lev was too thoughtful to notice the banter. "I think they want to borrow your expertise with European and

American business and diplomatic contacts."

"Okay, but why now? After all, I'm the newest and most junior member of PWZ's staff."

Both men knew the Israeli government was aware of the Islamic terror attacks aimed at Jack in both London and Israel. That was now old news. There had to be a more current reason for this summons.

"I think," Lev remarked slowly. "I think it may relate to the recent news from the PC-USA."

"The . . . ?"

"Presbyterian Church, USA. The meeting of their General Assembly."

Sternly, Jack returned, "You sure Bibi's got the right guy? I'm no theologian, much less an expert on Presbyterians."

Lev shook his head. "You're not being asked to comment on predestination! No, if my guess is right, what the PM's office cares about is the Middle East committee resolutions condemning Israel."

"Such as?"

"Such as calling Israel an apartheid state . . . such as demanding that realty companies not represent sales to Jewish clients in the settlement areas . . . such as pledging to oppose U.S. State and Federal efforts to do business with Israel. PC-USA . . . political correctness, run amok!"

"All of them passed?"

"No, a couple failed," Lev reported.

"That's good, anyway."

"The ones that failed," Lev corrected with a touch of bitterness, "didn't pass because either they weren't strong enough in condemning Israel or," he added with dripping sarcasm, "because they presumed to mention Hamas as a terrorist organization."

Jack frowned and bit his lip. "Serious?"

"As a heart-attack," Lev concluded. "A triple-order of Billy-Bob's chili-cheese-fries heart attack." His normal, cheerful face had reappeared.

"That's the man," Jack praised. "So, now what?"

"So get out of here and go see what they really want. Maybe you're being deported after all for stealing their prettiest girl. Go on. Get going."

✡ ✡ ✡

David Levin was an assistant to Israel's Director of Public Diplomacy and Media. He shook Jack's hand warmly and asked him to take a seat beneath a framed portrait of Netanyahu. Levin was a thin, forty-something man wearing round spectacles and a boyish grin.

"Thanks for coming," he said.

"What exactly do you do here?" Jack inquired, gesturing at the two desktop computer monitors and the three, wall-mounted television screens.

"The Prime Minister's office deals with four fronts," Levin explained, ticking off each on his fingers. "Military, diplomatic, home front, and public diplomacy. The last, my job, addresses how Israel is perceived on the world stage. So this is a different kind of warfare . . . no missiles or bullets . . . but still important to national security. I don't need to tell you how much bad press Israel gets, so we try to anticipate and counter it, as best we're able."

"Like?"

"We produce videos showing old people and children forced to take shelter from rocket attacks. We support websites in five languages. We have a new office of social media; a volunteer group of Israeli university students who are the most 'up' on current trends. For instance, do you have a Facebook account?"

"No," Jack admitted.

"Don't bother," Levin returned. "Our volunteers tell us nobody under twenty-five does anymore. Facebook use is down from eighty percent of everybody to sixty-five percent in just two years."

"Good thing that's not why you wanted to see me. Which brings me back to the point: why do you want *me*?"

Levin pushed his glasses back up on his short nose. "You heard about what happened with the Presbyterian Church USA General Assembly?"

So Lev had guessed correctly. "Only this morning. Lev Seixas clued me in. Political Correctness, eh? But that ship's already sailed, right? I mean, it's too late to affect those votes."

"Not exactly," Levin said. "A sub-committee from their Middle Eastern affairs group contacted us. They were tasked with following up the situation in Gaza and the settlement issue in light of the proposals. Sort of fact-checking after-the-fact, I'm afraid, but there it is."

"And you want me because . . . ?"

Once again, Levin counted out the rationale. "One: you're American, not Israeli. Two: even though you work for a pro-Israel organization, you're not a government employee. Three: you know the sentiment in Europe and so can offer a wider perspective on the issues. Four: when you first arrived in Israel you were on a sort of fact-finding mission yourself, yes?"

Jack agreed and Levin nodded in return.

"So. Five: you were personally a target of terrorism, which adds to your credibility."

"And what is it you want me to do, exactly?"

"Two delegates from the PC-USA are arriving tomorrow. Be their guide. Answer their questions truthfully, based on what you've seen yourself."

Jack paused for a moment's reflection. "Can Bette . . . Miss Deekmann . . . come along too?"

"Of course," Levin smiled. "We were hoping she would."

"All right, then," Jack said, standing. "I'm in."

18

Jack headed home to Dodi's. He parked, then dialed Bette's number. She did not pick up. It rang straight through and the voicemail was full. Had she seen it was him calling and just decided not to answer? What had he done wrong? Had he been too pushy? Had she changed her mind about sharing her innermost thoughts?

He told himself it didn't matter . . . but it did matter.

He told himself this didn't hurt . . . but it did hurt. Like a kid with a crush being ignored by the girl he adored, he ached inside for her company.

Jack rubbed his forehead and sat in the car a few more minutes. Orthodox pedestrians passed. A group of American tourists followed their guide up the street.

A sense of renewed loneliness gripped him; an empty longing he had not felt since the first months after he had buried his wife. This was no good. No good at all. If Bette didn't want to talk to him, Jack decided he would just wean himself away from her.

Jack pushed Bette's autodial on his phone. One, two, three rings and then, to his surprise, Bette answered cheerfully.

"Shalom, Jack."

It took him a beat to respond. He tried not to sound worried or hurt. "Well, hey . . . Bette. I've been trying to reach you. No answer."

"Sorry. I stepped out for cat food. Forgot my phone."

"Cat food! Okay. Okay, then! I'm glad . . . glad to hear your voice."

There was a pause. Bette asked, "Is everything okay? You sound . . . "

"I was just . . . "

"You sound stressed."

"I'm sorry. I was just . . . I've been asked to deal with a couple American pastors. No friends of Israel, I hear. So . . . "

"So . . . ?"

"So I was calling to ask . . . I need your help. One is a woman pastor. She might relate better to an Israeli woman." It was an excuse to see her again right away.

Jack knew it and so did Bette.

Another laugh. "Oh, Jack! So you hand her over to me, eh? I suppose if she gets too intense for me I can pretend I don't understand English."

Relief flooded through Jack. This was the Bette he knew. "Something like that."

"To tell you the truth, it's exhausting trying to make myself rest. What do you call it? Climbing the walls? A trip to get cat food was exciting."

"All right, then. I promise you will not be bored. At least, I think I can promise that."

"When?"

"Tomorrow?"

Bette's bubbling laughter was reward enough to make Jack smile.

✧ ✧ ✧

Even though there was a nice and reasonably priced hostel run by the Presbyterian Church less than half a mile from Old City Jerusalem, the visiting pastors had opted to stay instead at the Crowne Plaza, Tel Aviv. The high-rise hotel overlooking the Mediterranean was located on Gordon Beach.

Bette and Jack set out from Jerusalem at 6:00 a.m. in order to allow plenty of time to meet their charges at the requested appointment hour of 8:00. The Office of Public Diplomacy had furnished a spacious Mercedes ML 300

SUV limo for the day, but Jack was still more comfortable letting Bette do the driving.

The hotel lobby of the beachfront property was modern, stark, and drab. Only one of Jack's two charges was present, however.

"Glen Rankin," the pastor introduced himself. "San Diego."

Jack shook hands with the medium-height, forty-something pastor, balding and pudgy. "Jack Garrison," he said. "And this is Bette Deekmann. I'm American, but she's Israeli."

"A pleasure. My first time in Israel. I've been looking forward to the trip."

"I hope you have time around your official duties to experience the history," Bette offered.

"As do I," Rankin replied.

"Were we early?" Jack inquired. "There is one more coming?"

"Right on time," Rankin corrected. "My colleague, Pastor Sykes, is on a teleconference. She'll join us shortly, I'm sure. Ah . . . here she comes now."

From the bank of elevators that opened off the lobby came a plump, pleasant-looking, grandmotherly figure. She strode purposefully toward the waiting trio. "Time difference," she abruptly observed. "Had to give my assistant instructions before he goes to sleep. Have to be very specific with him so he doesn't mess things up. Brainless is not harmless, I always say. Shall we go?"

"Pastor Laura Sykes." Rankin's offered introduction was delivered behind the subject's back as she swept past Jack's outstretched hand and toward the exit.

When both pastors were settled in the back seat Jack tried again to be polite. "Jack Garrison," he said, pivoting to peer over the seatback.

"I know who you are, Mr. Garrison," Sykes responded. "I read the proceedings of the ECMP with great interest."

Oh-oh, Jack thought. "Then you know I'm no longer with that organization."

"Yes, and I know a little about the circumstances of your departure. Are you better now? Bit of a break-down, wasn't it?"

Regardless of what tales had been spread about him by his former anti-Semitic colleagues of the ECMP, Jack resolved to keep his cool. "I suppose so," he responded mildly. "I witnessed an Islamic terror attack here in Israel, and the Westminster Bridge attack in London."

Jack had three times been a target himself, but he did not voice this observation.

Sykes sniffed. "Must you be so pejorative? Leaping to condemn an entire religion for the acts of a few crazy people is so intolerant and leads only to more anger and resentment."

Glancing at Bette's hands clamped on the steering wheel and the set of her mouth, Jack knew she was struggling to maintain her composure as well. Discretely reaching over he patted her arm. *Stay calm,* the gesture said. "This is Bette Deekmann," Jack offered. "She's a Sabra."

"And how did you do your national service?" Sykes inquired.

"IDF," Bette retorted brusquely. "And then Border Police."

"Prison guards," retorted Sykes. "Well, listen. We don't want any sanitized, Jewish version of the truth about this apartheid state. Take us to a border settlement and let us see for ourselves."

"Exactly what I had in mind," Bette returned.

✡ ✡ ✡

Heading south from Jerusalem, the drive to Nirim, an Israeli community on Gaza's southeast corner, took them past Nahal Oz, site of some of the worst damage caused by incendiary kites launched by Palestinians. Bette gestured toward a scorched piece of earth alongside the highway. "Until a short time ago, that was a thriving wheat field."

Sykes harrumphed. "Looks like a poor job by the firefighters! In any case, you can't compare the loss of a few acres of grain to having to spend a lifetime in prison."

"This was the farmer's entire crop. Forty acres," Jack offered. "And yes, he can plant again next season, but for now *this* forty acres was his livelihood. And in defense of the firefighters," Jack added, "there have been four hundred and fifty such attacks since the flaming kite campaign started."

"Child's toys!" Sykes retorted. "Pinpricks against an elephant hide! How else can the oppressed make the world pay attention to their needs?"

"Wouldn't sitting down and negotiating be a better long term strategy?" Bette suggested. "Surely acts of terror serve to harden positions and not improve them?"

"Apartheid state!" Sykes asserted again. "The United Nations says inhumane acts, coupled with systematic oppression, and the complete domination of a minority race by the majority, equals *apartheid*. Hateful! But of course you don't read anything that's unfavorable to Israel, do you?"

"On the contrary," Jack corrected. "I read the original report you just cited. It was authored by a committee made up of Arab nations . . . and only Arab nations. The UN General Assembly did not approve the conclusions. And Ambassador Nikki Haley . . ."

"Ha!" Sykes erupted. "A puppet of the American-Israel alliance! Brainwashed pawn."

Smoothly Jack continued, "Ambassador Haley spoke to refute the charge that Israel is an apartheid state. There is no systematic oppression, there is no torture, and there is no imprisonment without trial. Arab-Israelis are full, voting citizens."

"Arab citizens are exempt from national service,"

Bette added, "though many of them still participate as volunteers."

"We're not speaking of Arab citizens of Israel, even though they too are treated as second-class citizens," Sykes countered. "Palestinians in Gaza are kept in . . . what's the quote? The largest open-air prison in the world."

"Stand by one," Jack replied. "Gaza is self-governing, as is the West Bank. The Palestinians in each enclave elected their leadership. If they aren't happy with the results, why blame Israel?"

"Because they are kept behind a fence at gunpoint! Even the sea is patrolled! What kind of a sovereign nation exists like that?"

"Perhaps one that exports terrorism to its neighbors," Bette returned. "If there were no terror attacks and no attempts by sea to run weapons and explosives into Gaza or launch them against the Israeli coast, there would be no need for a watchful presence. All my friends among the Border Police would rather be home with their families than facing rocks, bottles, Molotov cocktails, and rioters."

"I think this 'tour' may be a waste of our time." Pastor Sykes harrumphed again and retreated into a grumpy silence. Jack wondered if Pastor Rankin ever got to speak during one of these exchanges.

Pivoting, Jack looked over his other shoulder. The junior member of the fact-finding team was fast asleep, propped in the corner between headrest and window. His mouth was open and a little dribble of saliva painted its corner.

Following Jack's gaze, Sykes glanced at her colleague and smiled. "Poor, dear man. He is so very jet-lagged. We should keep our voices down, don't you think?"

✧ ✧ ✧

After leaving Highway 232, Bette maneuvered the Mercedes through the byways of the Negev until pulling into the parking lot of the Nirim kibbutz. "Why have you brought us here?" Sykes demanded, elbowing Rankin into a confused awakening.

"You see this landscape?" Jack asked. "When you think about settlements you picture Palestinian land forcibly occupied by new Jewish homes, yes? But Nirim has been here since 1946."

"Still an illegal seizure of Arab land!"

"Actually, not really," Bette corrected. "We are close to the Maon synagogue, which proves a Jewish presence here since the Sixth Century."

"Ancient history," Sykes protested.

"Historical facts should not be so easily discarded," Bette argued. "Another historical fact: there were no Palestinian people until 1948. There were Arabs living in the Ottoman Empire, or ruled by Transjordan after the end of World War I, but no independent Palestine . . .

ever."

"All the more reason to correct all the wrong-doing on the part of Israel over the last seventy years!"

Did Pastor Rankin ever have an independent thought? Jack wondered. *And if so, was he ever brave enough to voice it?*

Jack saw the muscles in Bette's shoulders tense. She was perfectly capable of going all *Krav Maga* . . . the Israeli no-holds-barred, use-any-weapon, take-no-prisoners, and go-in-for-the-kill martial art and attitude . . . but she resisted. With apparent great deliberation, she relaxed her muscles, beginning with her jaw.

When Bette resumed speaking, she sounded almost relaxed, and perfectly controlled. "Nirim is within the proposed United Nations boundary line drawn during the Partition proposal approved in 1947. However," she added, "it's only less than seven kilometers from the border with Gaza. Nirim's agricultural efforts go all the way up near the boundary . . . well, up to a sniper's distance from the boundary. They grow sweet potatoes and peanuts."

"I don't imagine you brought us all the way out here to demonstrate Israeli farming prowess," Sykes commented sarcastically.

"No, it's because there's someone here we want you to meet," Bette said. "Please, follow me."

A group of school age children playing on a trampoline stopped jumping long enough to stare at the visitors, then went back to their activity. Between two houses, a group of men drank wine and grilled steaks.

A pair of bicycles flanked the concrete walk leading up to the white-plastered, red-tile-roofed, ranch-style home. Bette knocked, and then called out a greeting in Hebrew.

A young woman in her late twenties opened the door. Smiling, she invited them in. "Lili Katz," Bette said, then pointed to a seated older woman holding a child on her lap. "This is Lili's mother, Alice, and Lili's son, four-year-old Benyamin." Bette then completed the introductions of Jack and the two pastors.

Since there weren't enough chairs in the small living room which incorporated the kitchen and a dining table, Alice and her grandchild excused themselves to an adjacent bedroom and shut the connecting door.

"I understand you'd like to speak with me about living here so close to Gaza, and how I feel about the border fence," Lili offered.

"Certainly, my dear," Sykes said politely. "And just when did you move here? Two years ago? Five?"

"Actually," Lili corrected. "I was born here. And my connection to Nirim goes even further back. My family were of the original settlers . . . *kibbutzniks* . . . in 1946. Of course the actual village was located in a different place, then."

"Why is that?" Sykes delved, as if already finding a weak spot to attack.

"Because in 1948 Nirim was on the direct route for

the invading Egyptian army. My grandfather was one of thirty-one defenders . . . who lived. We held them off," she said with quiet pride. "After the shelling, none of the homes were habitable. Besides, this second location gets slightly more rainfall. Water is life, you know."

"And what does your husband do?" Sykes inquired, sounding eager to change the subject. "Farming?"

"He did," Lili replied. "He was killed by a mortar shell launched from Gaza four years ago."

"I'm very sorry," Pastor Rankin offered. "Then why do you stay?"

He actually speaks! Jack thought.

"Actually," Lili said, "sometimes I wonder. Because it is home, I suppose. But ever since I was my son's age I have had nightmares about an Arab terrorist sneaking into my room with a knife."

"But nothing like that has happened here, has it?" Sykes prodded.

"No, not to me." Lili conceded.

Sykes sat back on the sofa and folded her arms across her chest.

"But the same year my husband was killed, Hamas terrorists came out of a terror tunnel near Kibbutz Sufa. That tunnel was over a mile long. I know we're further than that here but if they come out at night . . . "

"Don't you think the Palestinians should be treated more fairly than they have been?" Sykes probed. "Wouldn't that solve the problem?'"

"You speak as if we were arguing over someone not putting their trash cans away!" Lili protested. "Yes, most Palestinians want to raise their families in peace. This I believe. Palestinian workers helped my father build this house. My mother used to be a teacher. She had a Palestinian friend with whom she talked and shared lesson plans."

Lili shook her head sadly. "Not anymore. Hamas does not want peace. Palestinian Islamic Jihad does not want peace. Islamic terrorists want there to be no Israel at all . . . nothing else will satisfy them. Until then, we must have the fence. We must have border patrols. When I hear that thousands of Palestinians rush toward the barricade . . . " Lili shuddered, and then straightened upright. "Don't you know we would have to kill many, many more of them if they break through the fence? Now they launch burning kites . . . and still more rockets." Looking Sykes directly in the eye Lili said, "My son will go to school next year. Did you know that in our school there are no windows facing west?"

"Why is that?" Rankin blurted.

Surprised the junior pastor could be so ignorant, Jack was equally surprised when Sykes was the one who answered. "Supposedly, so snipers in Gaza can't shoot at children through them. Listen, my dear, thank you," the senior pastor said, standing up. "We've taken enough of your time. Goodbye, then. Think about moving your little one to a . . . to a less disputed place."

While Lili rocked her son, her mother walked their guests out to the SUV. "This is our home," Alice said bluntly, proving she had overheard the conversation even from behind the closed door. "Why should we have to leave? Besides, Nirim is three-quarters heaven. So if it's one-quarter hell . . . " She shrugged. "So be it."

✡ ✡ ✡

There was silence in the Mercedes for several minutes after leaving Nirim. Back on Highway 232, headed north, Jack finally broke the quiet. "If you have time, tomorrow we'd like to take you north."

"No, thank you," Sykes retorted sharply. "We have more important things to do. Tomorrow we meet with Rafa Husseini in Gaza to learn the reality of the humanitarian crisis Israel is perpetuating."

Back when Jack had been a part of the European Committee for Mid-East Policy he had also met with Rafa Husseini; he had also thought much the same as Pastor Sykes. *Everything was Israel's fault. Israel was the bully, battering the poor, abused Palestinians. There would be peace if only Israel treated the Palestinians fairly.* Remembering his own attitudes in those days, he struggled to be charitable with her willful blindness.

The difference between Jack and Pastor Sykes seemed to be that when Jack had come to Israel to see for himself, he became aware of how much misinformation . . . or outright lies . . . the Gentile world was ready to believe about the Jewish state. Sykes, on the other hand, would admit no possibility of any position in conflict with her own, preconceived views.

Still, Jack decided to continue trying. "Did you know that seventy-five per cent of Gaza's electricity comes from Israel?" he asked. "But in the recent riots . . . "

"Demonstrations!" Sykes corrected harshly.

Jack acquiesced. "In those . . . demonstrations . . . the Palestinians launched additional rocket attacks on the nearby Israeli towns. Unfortunately, their aim was off and they ended up knocking out a power station and blacking out thousands of their own citizens."

Sykes dismissed the point. "Israel is criminally slow about repairing the damage. It deliberately leaves those imprisoned in Gaza worse off than ever before."

Jack shook his head and glanced sideways at Bette. *You want to try?* his glance implored.

"You, of course, know about the Syrian refugee situation," Bette offered. "Syrians are caught between Bashir al-Assad's forces and many different rebel groups."

"One and a half million have fled to Jordan," Sykes agreed. "It is a humanitarian crisis of monstrously overlooked significance."

"Then, did you know that Jordan has closed its borders to additional refugees? Israel is helping resupply camps in southwest Syria, just across the Golan border. Tents, medical supplies, food. Israel has not only sent assistance, but is acting as a channel for supplies coming from Arab countries."

"Why haven't we heard of this in the West?" Rankin questioned.

"Arab governments who appear to cooperate with Israel face trouble from terrorists at home," Bette said, scanning the mirror and then pulling out to pass a slow-moving farm truck.

"A drop in the bucket for what's needed," Sykes argued. "Besides, the Golan was stolen from Syria in the first place."

"Here's one more thing you may not have heard about." Jack found himself deliberately ignoring Sykes' outbursts and focusing on Rankin alone. "Gaza has no seaport of its own. Israel is building docks on the island of Cyprus to act as a port for Gaza. When the new facility is operational it will vastly improve the shipment of goods to the people of Gaza."

"Under the control and snooping intervention of Israel," Sykes asserted.

"Isn't it reasonable for Israel to make sure that weapons and other contraband items are not arriving in Gaza? Weapons that would be used to kill Israeli citizens?"

"No sovereign nation should have to submit to such high-handed treatment!" Sykes retorted.

CHAPTER 18

Jack was more than frustrated. As far as Sykes was concerned, Israel was responsible for all that was wrong in the region. Further yet, even when Israel tried to do something helpful for its neighbors, it was either not enough, or carried out from some ulterior, oppressive motive.

Further conversation lagged until Bette directed the SUV off the highway at the town of Sderot. "I don't know about the rest of you, but I need a coffee," she said. Hearing no objection, after parking beside a stand of palm trees, Bette led the way into Café Marlowe.

Escorting the group past an upright piano decorated with a jar of daisies, Bette took them to an outside table and asked what they would like. When all the requests were made, Jack offered to get the drinks.

Seated in the pleasant shade of an umbrella Bette remarked, "Welcome to the Bomb Shelter Capital of the World. Parts of Sderot are only one kilometer from the Gaza border. The twenty-five thousand people who live here realize they have no more than fifteen seconds from the moment of hearing the siren to get to shelter. Sometimes as many as four rockets a day fall here."

"On land stolen from the Palestinians in 1948," Sykes returned without energy or emotion.

Jack reappeared with the coffee: two espresso cups and two blended, icy drinks. He had just set the tray down on the table when the air raid siren atop the adjacent apartment building began to wail.

"Time to go," Bette said. "Follow me."

"What? What?" Rankin burbled.

"Don't think!" Jack urged. "Move!"

Behind the line of palms in the parking lot was a concrete cubicle painted bright yellow on two sides and bright green on the other two. Bette, followed by Rankin, Sykes, and Jack, ducked inside. Stairs gave access to a concrete bunker under the parking lot.

At the head of the steps, just before descending, Jack glanced over his shoulder. A score of pedestrians, shoppers, and a mother stumbling as she pushed a baby carriage, all rushed toward the entrance. Ducking back outside, Jack helped the mom hoist the pram over the curb and inside the shelter door.

A loud whistling sound split the sky, seeming to come from right overhead. Instinctively, Jack ducked, just as the loud crump and reverberating boom of an impacting Qassem rocket arrived.

After the all clear sounded, Jack was not surprised that the two pastors opted to take their drinks 'to go.'

Back in the car, Sykes seemed compelled to go on the offensive. "Do you think that little demonstration will make me sympathetic to Israel? Besides the moral right of the Palestinian people to self-determination," she said, "there's also the matter of proportionate response. These back-yard rockets are almost toys, they are so inaccurate."

"You're saying if a child is killed by one it's almost accidental?" Bette demanded coldly. "An unfortunate casualty of what is just a demonstration of Palestinian frustration?"

Jack realized from Sykes' stony silence that those words accurately expressed her thoughts.

"Disproportionate response," Sykes repeated instead. "You know Israel will strike back with air raids, perhaps even a naval bombardment. Hundreds may die."

"Pastor Rankin," Jack said, ignoring Sykes once-and-for-all. "You're from San Diego, is that correct?"

"Imperial Beach, actually."

"So even closer to Tijuana than San Diego proper?"

Rankin agreed this bit of geography was correct. "About five miles or so."

"Now answer me this," Jack said. "What would you want the American government to do if a group of terrorists in Tijuana started lobbing missiles into Imperial Beach? Even if it was only one a day . . . even if nobody ever . . . well, hardly ever . . . got killed by it? If Mexico did not immediately deal with the problem, how long would you be willing to wait before demanding that America eliminate the threat once and for all?"

"Don't answer that preposterous hypothetical," Sykes ordered. Then, in a low voice but still audible within the car she said, "War monger. Zionist war monger."

There was no further conversation all the way back to Tel Aviv.

19

"What is *wrong* with those people?" Bette said to Lev. "*Boom*! They experience a Hamas rocket for themselves. Don't they know we could have all been killed? And they still act as if Israel caused it! Where are their heads?"

She and Jack sat with Lev on the courtyard of the Tmol Shilshom café and bookstore. They were meeting to unpack their report on the time spent with the PC-USA pastors.

"It didn't matter what we said . . . what we showed them . . . who they met," Bette lamented. "They came with the view that everything is Israel's fault and nothing would change . . . no, not even change. Nothing would make them even *admit* any other possibility!"

"Since you knew how their group voted before Sykes and Rankin came here," Jack reminded her, "did you really expect anything different? Don't you remember how I was when you first met me?"

"Perhaps you should not remind me!" Bette warned.

Lev enjoyed watching Jack and Bette debate. He refilled three glasses of *limonana* . . . lemonade mixed with crushed mint leaves . . . and remained silent.

"I thought Christians . . . American Christians anyway . . . all supported Israel," Bette concluded. "That woman was just so negative! She can act so kindly one minute, and sound so spiteful the next!"

While Bette continued to fume, Jack recounted the details of the trip to Nirim and the rocket attack in Sderot. "I don't think we accomplished anything," he concluded. "But since Sykes did most of the talking, I don't think we made anything worse." Lev stretched and brushed a fallen eucalyptus leaf off the table.

"You might be wrong," he offered.

Jack looked wounded.

"About not accomplishing something positive, I mean," Lev explained. "Mentioning terror attacks from across a nearby border to that San Diego pastor may affect him more than he let on."

Jack shook his head. "I doubt it. As far as he's concerned the example is just too preposterous to take seriously. Anyway, he'd be afraid to contradict Pastor Sykes!"

CHAPTER 19

Selecting an olive from a tray on the table Bette brandished it like a pointer and demanded, "Explain this to me: How is it that some American Christians are Israel's greatest supporters while others are the biggest foes?"

"What do you want first," Lev asked. "Politics or religion?"

"Politics," Bette said. "Easier for me to understand."

"Perhaps," Lev said. "Most evangelical Christian Americans are also politically conservative. They know Israel is a democracy with a tough, fair, independent court system. They know Israel is a true ally of America . . . maybe the only real ally in the Middle East."

"So why only evangelicals?"

With a glance at Lev, Jack took up the explanation. "Mainline churches are made up of social and political liberals. American liberals have always been pro-socialist and anti-business. Now that communism is a failed system, liberals still try to support what they term 'oppressed groups' by refusing to call terrorism what it is. Israel is the 'big bully preventing the Palestinians from achieving their national destiny.'"

"Rocket attacks don't matter? Suicide bombers don't matter? A commitment to wipe Israel off the map doesn't matter?" Bette blurted.

There was no possible reply to these queries. Neither Lev nor Jack attempted one.

Lev offered a plate with three kinds of cheese and three

kinds of bread, but Bette waved away the selection. "And politics was the *easier* thing to understand?"

"Easier to explain," Lev corrected. "*Understanding* is something else again."

"And religion?"

A passing breeze stirred the pink and white awnings rigged overhead.

"This is all you, Lev," Jack said.

Steepling his fingers together, Lev gathered his thoughts. "Way back before there was a modern Israel," he said, "even before the first Zionist congress . . . before Herzl . . . in 1891, an American named William Blackstone wrote a book called *Jesus is Coming.* Part of his belief system was that there had to be a Jewish nation here again. Today we would call him a Christian Zionist."

Jack whistled softly. "I'm impressed. Was he before his time? Did people think he was a nut?"

"Not at all," Lev said. "He got prominent Americans to pledge their support: J. P. Morgan, John D. Rockefeller, later even President Wilson. Of course Arthur Balfour in England. 1917. So far, okay?"

Jack looked at Bette, who nodded.

"Fast forward to 1948. So suddenly, there *is* an Israel again. All the Christians who believe in a Second Coming of Jesus are feeling vindicated because even the most unreligious types say the miracle of Israel is just that . . . miraculous, unexpected, significant. Israel's rebirth is sort of a down payment on the rest of End Times prophecy."

"Go on," Jack urged.

"1967. Israel retakes Old City Jerusalem. Another milestone. Great timing too, because evangelicals by the million buy, read, and believe a book called *The Late, Great Planet Earth.* Hal Lindsey. 1970. If you want to be on the right side of the Messiah . . . who doesn't, right . . . support for Israel is crucial. Supporting Israel grows even more amongst evangelicals as more books get written . . . *The Zion Chronicles* . . . and more prophecies get fulfilled. Jews come home to the land from Iran and Russia, from Ethiopia and Europe, from Latin America. Aided in making *Aliyah* by Gentiles . . . just like the Prophet Isaiah foretold."

"And the mainstream Christian churches are those who don't support the idea that Israel is a fulfillment of prophecy?"

Lev nodded. "Those like the National Council of Churches that refused to support Israel in the '67 war . . . mainline Christian churches . . . starting and promoting economic attacks on Israel like Boycott, Divest, Sanction."

Pausing, Lev let that information sink in.

"But there's more to it than that," he added. "Now there's a generation who haven't been taught the history, haven't studied the prophecy, haven't read the books. They may call themselves evangelicals, but they don't support Israel like their parents do."

"Really?" Jack wondered aloud.

"Really," Lev confirmed. "Recent studies show that Israel is regarded as one of the most powerful nations in the world . . . but power is not a quality that Millennials approve. They want 'friendly,' or 'culturally accessible,' or 'socially responsible.' In those categories Israel rates well below the middle when eighty countries are compared . . . even lower in some categories . . . and showing a huge drop in all the categories of favorability when you separate the Millennials from the older generations."

There was a painful silence. Finally, Jack asked, "So . . . what do we do now?"

Lev shrugged. "We keep doing what we're called to do. No more, but no less either."

✡ ✡ ✡

Jack couldn't sleep. He heard the clock behind Dodi's rocking chair in her living room strike 2:00 in the morning, then 2:15, and then 2:30. He felt like a colossal failure over his inability to make a difference . . . any difference at all . . . in the attitudes of the two American pastors from PC-USA.

Since coming to Israel, Jack had been drawn further and further into the significance of the land and its people. In dreams, visions, and personal encounters he had come to appreciate Israel's vital importance. God . . . the God of the promises to Abraham, Isaac, and Jacob . . . was still intimately and powerfully involved with this little scrap of earth.

Jerusalem was still the Holy City . . . the crossroads of the world . . . ground zero in the ultimate battle between good and evil . . . the point of the return of Yeshua ha Mashiach; Jesus the Messiah.

How was it possible for Christians . . . pastors, even . . . to say they love God and then not love His original Chosen People?

As for the prospects for peace requiring Israel to stop being a bully, Jack had seen enough to recognize the truth of the cliché: 'If the Arabs lay down their weapons there will be peace. If Israel lays down its weapons, there will be no Israel.'

Even while admitting and lamenting the lot of the Palestinians, why couldn't observers like Sykes and Rankin also admit Israel's predicament? What was wrong with them?

How had Lev explained it? *Most of them are good-hearted, well-intentioned folks, but they substitute a gospel of social justice for the Gospel of Jesus. They don't believe in miracles. When they think of Jesus feeding the five thousand with five loaves and two fish, they say Jesus just guilted the people into sharing what they had hoarded for themselves. They do not anticipate that Jesus will literally, physically return. They expect that good deeds and proper attitudes will bring about a paradise on earth. If they think at all about the promises to Israel, they quickly substitute 'the Church' for 'Israel.'*

Sometimes they even think 'the Church' is the same as, 'It doesn't matter what you believe, as long as you're sincere.' Replacement theology. Of course, when you start replacing one bit of scripture with your own understanding, pretty soon you get Moses receiving the Ten Suggestions on Mount Sinai, and Jesus saying of Himself that He was A way, A Truth, and A version of Life, instead of The *Way,* The *Truth, and* The *Life.*

There had come a moment in the conversation with Lev and Bette when the spiritual water had gotten too deep for Bette, so the discussion concluded. Later, Jack phoned Lev to continue expressing his frustration and his desire to have more to offer.

Just as the two friends rang off for the evening, Lev had offered one last bit of encouragement. "You do realize," Lev said, "that even what you experienced with the American pastors is itself a fulfillment of prophecy."

"How do you figure that?" Jack asked.

"Listen to what Saint Paul says to Timothy in his second letter. Writing about what Paul calls the 'last days,' he says: *'For men will be lovers of themselves, lovers of money, boasters, proud, blasphemers, disobedient to parents, unthankful, unholy, unloving, unforgiving, slanderers, without self-control, brutal, despisers of good, traitors, headstrong, haughty, lovers of pleasure rather than lovers of God, having a form of godliness, but denying its power.'*"

"Ouch!" Jack said. "You're telling me this to encourage me? But I get it: time is short and Jesus is coming back soon? But hasn't every age since Jesus thought their time was the worst?"

"You tell me," Lev challenged. "Don't you see a sort of escalation in things? How about the very last line: 'having a form of godliness, but denying its power?' Remind you of anyone?"

"So what do I do differently? What do I say?"

"Jack," Lev returned, "did it ever occur to you that it isn't up to you? Your job is to say 'yes' when God puts you in a certain spot and then wait for God to guide the words. Jesus says, '*When they arrest you and deliver you up, do not worry beforehand or premeditate what you will speak. But whatever is given you in that hour, speak that; for it is not you who speak, but the Holy Spirit.*' Don't you think that same freedom from anxiety should apply to being judged by two pastors of the Politically Correct USA?"

The end of that phone call had come three hours earlier, but Jack was still wrestling with what he could have said differently; what he could have done better. He prayed for a visit with Eliyahu; a dream, a vision, another deepening of his understanding. No supernatural appointment answered him and eventually, he slept.

20

Sipping chilled pomegranate juice while Dodi made a charcoal sketch of a basket of fruit, Jack silently named each variety he noticed in the overflowing container. There were grapes, cherries, plums, oranges, tangerines, dates, avocados, and one unknown specimen, whose skin was yellow-orange shaded with pink, and which looked like a spiny, oversized egg.

"What's that one?" he asked abruptly. "Sorry. Didn't mean to interrupt your concentration."

"No matter." Following the line of his gaze she laughed. "You don't know *tsabbar*? Prickly pear?"

"Cactus fruit? You eat it? I thought that was just in old John Wayne movies where the wagon train is lost and starving."

Laying down the plump charcoal stick and dusting her hands Dodi said, "Good thing you asked me and not Bette! *Tsabbar* . . . sabra! It's how native-born Israelis refer to themselves."

"Sabra! I heard Bette use it. Of course I knew that meaning . . . but not where the word came from."

"Grows on the hills. Prickly on the outside . . . sweet on the inside."

Jack mentally agreed he was relieved to have exposed his ignorance to his grandmother and not first to Bette. She would have thought he was teasing.

Hanging on the wall behind Dodi's easel were a number of framed photographs. One was of a rabbi in IDF uniform. In one hand, he held a prayer book and under his arm, he clasped a Torah scroll. Around him were other soldiers, one of whom was blowing a shofar.

Another photograph was the famous snapshot of three wide-eyed Israeli paratroopers standing in front of the Western Wall immediately after the liberation of Old City Jerusalem in 1967. "You said Sol was in the '67 war too?" he asked.

Dodi smiled and unfolded a magazine from a hamper beside her stool. On its cover were three men . . . much older than the ones depicted in the '67 photo . . . standing in the same spot. "Haim, Itzik, and Zion recreated the pose for the fiftieth anniversary," she said. "But you're wrong in one way. David Rubinger took the famous picture. Mine were taken by Sol. The angles are slightly different you see."

"I remember you said he was there. On the spot."

"Sol was in charge of the security detail for Yossi Ronen, the radio journalist. Sol was right beside him all the way, and right there, next to Sol, is Bette's grandfather, David ben Elijah. The man with the Torah scroll is Rabbi Goren. Back then he was Brigadier General Goren." Dodi studied the 1967 images for a long moment, sighed heavily, then picked up her stick of vine charcoal and resumed sketching.

Jack peered into the expressions Sol Baruch had captured in 1967. What were those young men feeling? Amazement, exultation, fear? Their faces were shadowed by brows of their helmets, and the rows of stone rising over their heads glowed much, much brighter. He examined the face of David ben Elijah; a man who had seen such suffering . . . son of a rabbi . . . descended from rabbis. There was still so much unanswered about his life.

✡ ✡ ✡

Tourists streamed past the small café on the Via Dolorosa where Bette and Jack met with Simon Gross.

The art historian raised his brows in an expression of awe, nodded at Jack, and then slid the carefully packaged, stained-glass medallion across the table to Bette. "This is indeed a treasure. But of course you must know this." Simon leveled his gaze at Bette and gently tapped the package.

She smiled slightly. "It has been a treasure in *my* family. My grandfather brought it with him from a synagogue destroyed in Germany. He rescued it during the holocaust."

Simon cleared his throat and leaned closer, across the table. "Very similar in style and color to Augsburg Cathedral. Late eleventh century. It is in the heart of Bavaria. Created in a time when people could not read, and so the pictures in the windows told the Bible stories. Portraits of Abraham, Moses and others."

"My grandfather's synagogue was in Nuremburg. Destroyed during *Krystalnacht*, 1938. He was a young man. His father, my great-grandfather, remained behind. He didn't survive."

"Do you know how your grandfather selected this shard to preserve?"

"I think it was a random choice."

"Then perhaps it was divinely selected *for* him." Simon produced a packet of papers. "Here are my conclusions. I'll sum it up, and then you may study further. The image is from a window showing the story of Abraham's sacrifice of his son Isaac. You have the tip of the ram's horn; the ram which the Lord provided as the substitute sacrifice for Isaac. Examined closely you see briars and thorns wrapped around the ram's horn. The thorns and the brambles are made up of an almost microscopic pattern of engraved Hebrew scripture references; mostly Micah 3:12 through 4:13. The prophecy that in the last days the Lord's Temple will be established and people will stream to it."

Then Simon added, "And Micah proclaims '*Rise and thresh, O Daughter of Zion.*' There are other prophetic references within the image as well. I've listed them for you."

Bette said, "I don't think my grandfather knew there were scriptures coded in the glass."

Simon explained. "The entire image is made up of the words of the story." He lamented, "I can only imagine what secrets the entire window must have contained."

"I have this much at least." Bette tucked the package into her satchel.

Simon narrowed his eyes in thought, "May I ask you if your great-grandfather held any position of authority in the synagogue?"

"He was the rabbi. Sephardic community. A very long history in the Diaspora. My grandfather would have inherited his position."

Simon was silent a long moment. "Well, then," he said as if that explained everything.

"Yes?"

"And now there's you . . . for such a time as this," Simon concluded.

———————————   ✧ ✧ ✧   ———————————

A three-ring binder contained forty pages of photographs and Simon's notes about the ancient stained glass medallion. Bette, Jack, and Lev added two leaves to Bette's kitchen table, yet it still was not large enough to contain all the material when unbound.

Lev laid out the original Hebrew text and a half-dozen different English Biblical translations and commentaries, each opened to the book of the prophet Micah. The intricate strokes of Hebrew script that made up the shading and the image of the ram's horn were distinct and precise beneath the glow of a magnifying lamp.

Simon's notes told them where to begin their examination of the artifact. The spiral tip of the ram's horn contained these words: "Abraham answered, '*God Himself will provide the lamb . . . my son.*'"

Lev studied the inscription. "It's a fragment of scripture only, but points us clearly to Genesis, Chapter 22."

"The story of Abraham offering his only son, Isaac, to God," Jack remarked as he opened a Bible to the reference, and slid it toward Bette. "Abraham offering Isaac to God happened right here at the location of the Temple Mount."

Bette read aloud. "He bound his son Isaac and laid him on the altar, on top of the wood. Then he reached out his hand and took the knife to slay his son. But the Angel of the Lord called out to him from heaven, *'Abraham! Abraham!'* 'Here I am,' he replied.

"*'Do not lay a hand on the boy,'* God said. *'Do not do anything to him. Now I know that you fear God, because you have not withheld from me your son, your only son.'*

"Abraham looked up, and there in a thicket he saw a ram caught by its horns. He went over, took the ram, and sacrificed it as a burnt offering instead of his son. So Abraham called that place, *The Lord Will Provide.* And to this day it is said, 'On the mountain of the Lord it will be provided.'"

"The Mountain of the Lord," Jack repeated.

"Jerusalem," Bette whispered in awe.

Jack added, "And on the Mountain of the Lord, God provided His only son, Jesus, named *Yeshua* in Hebrew, as the final sacrifice."

Bette replied in awe, "*Yeshua* means Salvation."

Lev leaned close toward the image in the mag light. "Now look! The next words inscribed in the medallion! *'In the last days the mountain of the Lord's Temple will be established and chief among the mountains; it will be raised above the hills, and peoples will stream to it!'*"

Inscribed fragments of the Last Days prophecies from Micah, Chapter 4, foretold the rebuilding of the Holy

Temple and the ingathering of the Jewish people after
a time of suffering and exile. It seemed clear to the trio
Micah had been writing about this very hour of history.

Lev read: *"'In that day, declares the Lord, I will gather
the lame, I will assemble the exiles and those I have brought to
grief . . . The Lord will rule over them in Mount Zion from that day
and forever . . . Now many nations are gathered against you. But they
do not know the thoughts of the Lord; they do not understand His
plan. He who gathers them like sheaves to the threshing floor . . . Rise
and thresh, O Daughter of Zion . . . you will break to pieces many
nations.'"*

Jack nodded. "Does anyone remember anymore that
Solomon's Temple was built on the threshing floor which
King David bought from Araunah?"

Lev traced the line of letters winding through the
pattern of thorns around the ram's horn. "There's so
much in the inscriptions! The size of a man's palm! So
much more! But look! Jack! Look at this one! Here it is," he
remarked. "The reference from Micah 5:2. The prophecy
that Messiah will be born in Bethlehem, where David the
shepherd of Israel was born. *'But you, Bethlehem Ephrathah,
though you are small among the clans of Judah, out of you will come
for me one who will be ruler over Israel, whose origins are from of
old, from ancient times.'"*

Bette smiled softly. "Messiah's birth place is in the book
of Micah? How could I not know this? Bethlehem? Where
Jesus was born in a lambing cave among the shepherds?

Bethlehem, where every little shop sells olive wood nativity sets!" She laughed aloud in wonder. "Well, it's all here, for everyone in Israel to see, isn't it? Here for me. Hidden in plain sight."

Jack tried to order his racing thoughts. Within these scriptures, etched into a shard of glass and rescued from the destruction of the holocaust, was the story of Israel and salvation, from beginning to end.

"Did your grandfather know what he had?"

"A treasure. That's what my family called it. Generations of rabbis in my family. I assumed the medallion was treasured because it was a remnant of our exile, brought home to Israel when the nation was reborn."

Lev questioned. "You're saying he didn't know what he carried home?"

Bette answered, "I don't know if he knew. I mean . . . Jesus? That is the name of a Gentile. But when you say Messiah is born a Jew in Bethlehem. A Jew named *Yeshua.* Salvation. And when you see that on the Mountain of the Lord, God provided the lamb for Abraham's sacrifice! Then I understand!" Bette's eyes brimmed. "Perhaps only now in these last days these things can be revealed to us."

21

"My grandfather mentioned Sol several times in his correspondence," Bette explained to Dodi. "Your husband served with him in the IDF."

"Yes. David ben Elijah. He and Sol fought together in 1948 when the Old City was lost, and for the years that followed; right the way through. They were together when the Old City was recaptured. Together at the Western Wall when the shofar was blown. Dear friends and comrades."

"Then surely my grandfather would have told Sol about this."

Bette unwrapped the medallion and passed it to Dodi as Jack looked on.

The old woman's face lit up with surprise and delight. "Oh, my dear! Yes! Yes of course!" She picked it up by the chain and let the light glitter on the glass.

"You recognize this?" Jack was amazed.

"Of course," Dodi exclaimed. "Sol made the bezel, you see!" She touched the gold ring surrounding the glass. "Your grandfather gave him the instructions. What he wanted it to say. The words engraved on it."

"Do you know what it means?" Bette asked. "It seems very important, somehow."

Dodi adjusted her reading glasses and studied the inscription. "Threshing floor. And these passages of scripture. The Temple Mount was a threshing floor in the time of King David. But what does it mean? On a personal level, perhaps it is a reference to David's personal suffering? Or the suffering of Israel? Threshing floor. It's a sort of metaphor for life. We are beaten and go through suffering to discover our strength—our worth, you see? As wheat stalks are threshed to separate the stalks from the grain, and then the worthless chaff is separated from the grain, perhaps? But beyond that I can't think of the significance."

"How did Sol come to make the bezel?"

"He was learning the art of jewelry-making in those days. This task was a favor to a friend."

Bette thanked Dodi and slid the precious medallion back into its protective pouch.

CHAPTER 21

The deeper meaning still seemed far from reach.

——————————— ✡ ✡ ✡ ———————————

Jack woke with a start and peered around his darkened bedroom in Dodi's house. Had he heard a noise? Had there been a bumping sound, or was it just part of the confused dream he'd been having?

Scooping up his wristwatch from the bedside table, he thumbed the button to illuminate the display: 4:30. Somewhere in a nearby tree, a night bird offered a soft cry: *Hoop-hoo, Hoop-hoo.*

There was no other sound except for the slow dripping of the bathroom faucet, which Jack had promised to fix but had so far failed to fulfill. Swinging out of bed, Jack padded silently down the hall. Dodi's gentle, even breathing, complete with its slight wheeze, convinced him she was sound asleep.

Nevertheless, Jack continued the rounds of the place, rattling door handles and checking window latches. Everything was secure.

He found himself in Dodi's studio. Clipped to her easel was the 1967 photograph of Sol, David ben Elijah, and the rabbi with the Torah scroll. What had Dodi said the rabbi's name was? Goren, Jack thought. A half-life-sized charcoal rendering of the scene was Dodi's current project.

For being in a darkened room, there was a surprising

amount of light in her sketch. From the upraised shofar at the upper left of the frame, a pale streak extended diagonally across the gleam of the prayer book pages and descended to the polished handles of the Torah scroll where they protruded beneath Goren's embrace.

Hoop-hoo, said the night bird gently.

A faint humming sound, like the buzz of a radio receiver in-between stations caught Jack's attention. It seemed to be coming from the photo, from the charcoal enlargement, or perhaps from them both. Leaning closer Jack thought he could make out words: "This is Yossi Ronen reporting. We are now walking on one of the main streets of Jerusalem towards the Old City. The head of the force is about to enter the Old City."

Jack touched beads of perspiration on his forehead, though the night was cool. The crackling sounds evolved from a poorly tuned radio to the sound of distant gunfire.

Distant, Jack thought. *About fifty years distant.*

Then Jack was in 1967, jogging alongside a slightly built man with a close-cropped beard in military gear. In that figure, Jack recognized a half-century-younger version of David ben Elijah. And with him, Sol Baruch.

The Mount of Olives reared up near them. The northeastern corner of the Old City wall loomed beside them. Gunfire popped and sputtered. A file of Jewish soldiers, careful to maintain twenty feet of separation as they ran so as to minimize the casualties from a sniper or a grenade, sprinted past a burned out Jordanian bus.

"The Lions Gate!" Sol murmured with barely suppressed excitement. "We're the first into the Old City, David! Nineteen years since they drove us out!"

Then they were on the Temple Mount. Up ahead was the Dome of the Rock. "Where is the Western Wall?" David asked urgently. "How do we get there?"

"Follow me," Sol offered.

Suddenly Jack saw Bette! Dressed in her IDF uniform, she was beside her grandfather . . . and she wore the medallion!

A radio operator's wireless crackled to life. *All Forces stop firing! Repeat: Stop firing. Protect every building. Do not touch any of the holy places.*

Jack tried to call to Bette, but she neither heard nor saw him.

Still jogging, the squad passed the spot where the Temple of Solomon had stood, where Judah Maccabee had presided over the Temple's cleansing, where generations of High Priests had entered the Holy of Holies once each year, where Jesus had taught and celebrated the Feast of Dedication, where the veil had been rent in two at Jesus' death.

Past where Araunah's threshing floor, purchased by King David for all those future uses, though lying beneath the dust of centuries, still presented the presence of the Angel of Lord suspending judgment and sparing the Holy City.

The reporter continued his breathless recital of their progress: "I'm walking right down the steps towards the Western Wall. I'm not a religious man, I have never been, but this . . . this is the Western Wall. I'm touching the stones of the Western Wall!"

A man Jack recognized as the one Dodi called Rabbi Goren appeared as Jack had seen him in photo and painting: brigadier general's uniform, Torah scroll, prayer book. Goren handed a shofar to a soldier. *"Baruch atah Hashem, menachem tsion u-voneh Yerushalayim."*

Blessed art Thou, Who comforts Zion and rebuilds Jerusalem.

Hatikva, the Hope, Israel's national anthem, rose from the emotionally constricted throats of the soldiers: "As long as within our hearts the Jewish soul sings, as long as forward, to the East, looks the eye . . . Our hope is not yet lost. It is two thousand years old, to be a free people in our land: the Land of Zion and Jerusalem!"

"We're going to pray now for our fallen soldiers," Goren commanded, "in the words *Aluf Alufim* Judah Maccabee prayed: *'Merciful Lord in heaven, may the heroes and the pure . . . who fell in this war against the enemies of Israel, who fell for their loyalty to You . . . who fell for the liberation of the Temple, the Temple Mount and Jerusalem, the City of the Lord . . . be under Thy Divine wings.'"*

Even though it was a vision . . . or a dream . . . Jack shivered. The words were exactly the same offered by Judah Maccabee in Jack's vision of the cleansing of the

Temple . . . two thousand years earlier. What had Jack heard? Sometimes the Jews have to fight to receive the land, sometimes to keep the land . . . but also, sometimes to reclaim it, even if that recapture also required repentance and purification. From the sons of Jacob, to the armies of Joshua; from the mighty men of David to Judah the Hammer and his brothers . . . the soldiers of Israel of 1948 and 1967 and today were the genetic and spiritual descendants of all those heroes who had gone before.

Bette removed the medallion and held it aloft, catching the light.

Sunlight blasted through the glass, projecting scriptures and moving images on the wall. Here, above the profiles of Sol and David and Rabbi Goren, was Abraham sacrificing the ram, and King David on the threshing floor, calling out to God. King Solomon dedicated the Temple, and a towering menorah illuminated Judah Maccabee's face.

And then . . . at last . . . Jesus carried the cross on his back . . . surrounded by multitudes crying, *"Blessed is He Who comes in the Name of the Lord!"*

Rabbi Goren continued the prayer of Judah the Hammer: *"The Lord being their heritage, may they rest in peace, for they shall rest and stand up for their allotted portion at the End of Days. And let us say: Amen."*

"Amen!" was shouted by a hundred IDF voices, punctuated by distant rifle shots. For just a brief instant, the Israeli troopers coalesced into the exact photographic image snapped in 1967. They looked so lost in wonder and so caught up in the drama Jack thought they didn't even realize a picture had been taken.

Goren traded the prayer book for the shofar and blew a loud, piercing blast. Again and again, the stones of Jerusalem echoed to the ancient ram's horn signal.

"Le shana Hazot be Yerusalayim," Goren shouted. "This year in a rebuilt Jerusalem. In the Jerusalem of old!"

Three days and nights passed since the vision of Rabbi Goren and the retaking of Jerusalem in 1967. Jack went to bed expectantly each night, hoping Eliyahu would appear in the darkness and show him the meaning of it all.

What came next? Could he not also bring Jack into the future?

Tonight Bette came to dinner and Dodi put the final touches on her latest painting. She was cleaning her paintbrushes when Jack and Bette entered the studio.

Neither had seen the completed work.

She looked up at them and smiled, her eyes crinkling at the corners. "Would you like to see it now?"

"Are you ready?" Jack asked.

"It's finished." She motioned for him to come around the easel.

A beam of light illuminated the canvas. Jack gasped and Bette put her hand to her mouth as they took in the sight of Rabbi Goren at the wall, holding the shofar to his lips. There, in the crowd of Israeli soldiers surrounding the rabbi, were the faces of Sol and David ben Elijah as Jack had witnessed them in the vision.

Eliyahu's visage, and Jack's own face, were present in the rank behind the soldiers.

Jack exclaimed, "But how?"

Bette pointed a trembling finger at the image. "This is . . . it is very like . . . I saw this in a dream!"

Now Jack turned his astonished gaze toward Bette. "But I had this vision . . . and you . . . you, Bette . . . you were in it."

Dodi answered quietly, "I thought perhaps you both might. Now look again, more closely, at the stones of the wall."

Above Rabbi Goren were translucent projections of men cast on the roughhewn stones. The Ark of the Covenant stood in the center of the ancient threshing floor. Surrounding it were the faces of Abraham, Isaac, and Joseph. Moses stood beside King David and King Solomon and Judah Maccabee.

"Yes!" Jack sank slowly onto a chair. He was unable to tear his attention from the faces of real men; visions he knew well. "But how do you know these men? How? You painted them. And . . . that's . . . Eliyahu? And the others?"

Dodi sat beside Jack. "It is written, '*Your old men will dream dreams and your young men shall see visions.*' I know them as well as I know my own face."

"I have seen visions. *And* dreamed dreams," Jack mumbled.

"And I, too!" Bette insisted.

"Yes," Dodi said matter-of-factly. "Now I will tell you: They are as real as you and I. They are as real as we are in this moment. Past, present, and future, all is connected, and all is leading to the moment when the Temple will be rebuilt on the ancient threshing floor once again."

"It's going to happen soon, isn't it?"

Dodi nodded. "From the moment Rabbi Goren blew the shofar, we knew the time was near. Jack, do you know the meaning of the Rabbi's name? Rabbi Goren. *Goren* means, in Hebrew, 'Threshing Floor.'"

"Bette! That's it!" Jack exclaimed. "The message: 'Hear Goren!' They heard the rabbi named Threshing Floor proclaim the rebirth of Jerusalem's Temple on the Threshing Floor!"

✡ ✡ ✡

The tapping at Jack's bedroom door increased in frequency and intensity, snapping him out of a confused dream. In his nightmare, terror attacks in London and Jerusalem were both carried out while Jack was powerless to stop them.

"Jack? Jack, dear?" Dodi's voice called out to him. "There's someone outside the gate saying he wants to speak with you."

"What? Who?" Jack wondered if his words were as slurred as his thoughts. He fumbled for his watch on the bedside table. Six in the morning! "Did he give his name?"

"I couldn't understand it and the little television screen is all blurry so I can't really see clearly. Were you expecting anyone?"

"No," Jack said. "But I'm awake. I'll come."

Padding toward the entryway in his bare feet Jack wondered who could be calling so early. On top of that question, Jack wondered who even knew where to find him. Apart from Lev and Bette, not many in Israel knew that Jack had moved in with his grandmother.

At the moment, his hand touched the latch a chill prickled the back of Jack's neck. The lock clicked and the gate swung open even as his mind shouted a warning.

Too late! The entry was open.

Pudgy, apologetic features greeted Jack's worried scowl. Pastor Rankin stood under the sweep of a jacaranda branch. A folded newspaper was under his arm. "Good morning," the preacher offered. "Shalom. Sorry to be calling so early. Hope you don't mind. Jet lag, you know. Been awake for hours and finally couldn't wait any longer.

Truthfully, I wasn't sure how hard this place would be to find. Want me to go away and come back? If you could tell me where to get coffee, I don't mind waiting 'til later."

Jack leaned forward to peer more closely at the speaker. Was this really the same man? In just thirty seconds outside Dodi's courtyard Pastor Rankin had spoken more words than in all the entire day he and Jack had ridden in the limo together. "No, of course not," Jack said, pushing open the gate. "Come in. We'll have coffee here. Have a seat," he offered, gesturing toward a patio table. "Back in a minute."

Dodi had already anticipated the need and put an electric kettle of water on to boil. Jack returned to the preacher with a French press coffee maker and two mugs. "Hope you drink it black," he said. "So, Pastor Rankin, tell me how you found me."

"Please! Call me Glen. Actually, it wasn't that hard. You see, I didn't know until yesterday that your grandmother is Dodi Baruch. *The* Dodi Baruch. I love her paintings! I have a couple reproductions. The one of Jesus in the bow of the boat calming the storm is my favorite! Hangs in my church office. When I added it up, I knew you could help me. Anyway, I spoke with the Public Diplomacy office and they directed me to Lev Seixas and after I explained to him why I wanted to contact you, he told me where to find you."

Rankin paused as if everything was now clear.

"And why exactly *do* you need to find me? What sort of

help can I offer?"

Rankin nodded. "I went to the wall . . . the Western Wall, you know? While I was there, something happened to me. I can't explain it, but . . . maybe you know what I mean?"

Jack nodded encouragement.

Unfolding the newspaper, the pastor spread it out on the table. "My hotel gets international papers," he said. "This is one I found in the lobby as I was coming to see you."

It was a copy of the British tabloid, *The Guardian*. Above the inside fold was a headline reading: 'Israeli Forces Kill Another Palestinian Protestor.' The article was accompanied by a photo showing teenagers with Palestinian flags grouped around a body on the ground as tear gas shells rained around them.

Jack grunted. "Did you come to lecture me about what a bully Israel is? Because Pastor Sykes already did that pretty thoroughly."

"No, no!" Rankin objected. "That's not it! See, I was there. This headline is a lie."

"What do you mean?"

"I saw it happen! We . . . Pastor Sykes and I . . . we were watching what was supposed to be a peaceful protest. Then I saw this kid messing with something on the ground . . . lighting something. Then he was running toward the border fence, raising it like he was getting ready to throw it . . . when it exploded! The Palestinian security men hustled us away from there right away!"

Slowly, pondering what to say, Jack tapped the paper and remarked, "*The Guardian* has always had an anti-Israel bias. Living in London, I read it on the Tube every morning. Even if they know the truth . . . "

"But that's not it!" Rankin insisted. "Before I saw this paper! The Palestinian guards told us: 'Wasn't it terrible how Israel killed that boy? Did you see how they killed that peaceful protestor?' Then Pastor Sykes said, 'Terrible. Terrible! Israel has so much to answer for!'"

Rankin paused. Caught in the emotion, he was shaking. "The world is so ready to blame Israel! That's what you were trying to tell us."

"So . . . Pastor Rankin," Jack asked.

"Glen, please. Glen."

"Glen," Jack repeated. "What do you want from me?"

"I changed my plane reservation. Told Pastor Sykes I was staying a few more days. Please . . . start over. Tell me again about Israel and prophecy."

Dodi entered the courtyard, carrying a framed picture with its back to the men.

Rankin stood and bobbed his head. Mrs. Baruch," he said. "So pleased to meet you. I'm such an admirer of your work."

"I hope you don't mind, but I couldn't help overhearing the conversation," Dodi said, "but I think you'll find this painting relates to what you were asking." When the picture's subject was revealed, it was a portrait of Jesus, wearing the crown of thorns. Behind him, outlining him amid a sky full of stars was a Star of David. "It's called 'Son of David,'" she explained. "Funny how so many people forget Jesus was first of all Jewish! The Jewish Messiah, before there even were any Gentile Christians."

"That's what I'm talking about," Rankin agreed.

Without revealing the visions and dreams which Jack had seen, he and Dodi spent the next two hours recounting for Glen Rankin why Israel remained central to God's plan for the human race. "I want to stress that I was every bit as hostile . . . as ready to blame Israel for the lack of peace . . . as you," Jack confessed. "Little-by-little, over time, I came to really experience God's love for this land . . . for the ones who remain His original Chosen People. I now believe . . . even if I don't fully understand . . . that God's promises are forever. Those promises include His commitment to bless those who bless Abraham and His descendants, but also to curse those who curse those same descendants."

"That's what I felt when I put my hand on the wall," Glen Rankin agreed. "There's an energy there . . . like a couple thousand years of prayers and longing for a homeland are stored up there." He frowned and his chin dropped.

"Something still bothering you?" Dodi inquired, offering to refill the pastor's coffee.

Rankin waved away the coffeepot. "Back home." He began slowly, choosing his words and grimacing as if sensing an obnoxious taste in his mouth. "My colleagues, I mean. They all believe Israel is a racist, oppressive, apartheid state. They think they are doing God's work when they promote Boycott-Divest-Sanction. Punish Israel until Israel . . . I don't know what . . . behaves?"

"Ceases to exist," Jack concluded. "But listen, it isn't just among your denomination. A lot of the so-called 'liberal thinkers,' from all around the world, agree with BDS."

Rankin's head bobbed. "So here's another issue: I now think many of them believe Christianity is a philosophy of doing good . . . but they want it . . ."

"Without a Jewish Jesus," Dodi offered, gesturing at her painting.

"That's it exactly," Rankin agreed. "They've heard and bought into the notion that Israel so oppresses the weak Palestinians that there's no room to see the One the story is really about. Before I can get them to even consider scripture . . . especially prophecy . . . how can I combat the attitudes about modern Israel? You know: politics, economics, fences and walls . . . "

"It's tough," Jack admitted, "but not impossible. Remember: what you've heard about Israel is a lie. So the way to refute a pack of lies is with the truth."

"But not truth supplied by a pro-Israel website or

newspaper," Rankin protested. "They'd just laugh at me . . . or worse."

"No, I was thinking about offering to take you around and let you see for yourself."

Rankin's face beamed. "That is exactly what I hoped you'd say! There's just one more thing . . . "

"Yes?"

"When I told Pastor Sykes, she insisted on coming with me."

Jack felt his face contort as if he had bitten into a particularly sour lemon.

"Thought I needed to be protected from Israeli brainwashing," Rankin continued. "Is it alright?"

"Of course," Dodi replied before Jack could frame a response. "And I will come as well . . . and we'll ask Bette Deekman to join us, shall we?"

What could Jack do but agree? "Give me time to phone Bette," he said.

⸙ ⸙ ⸙

"Yes, of course I'll come," Bette agreed. "But I heard you say 'north,' Jack," Bette recalled. "What exactly does that mean? Where are we headed?"

Jack swallowed hard. "Driving to Ariel. Lon Silver's place."

Bette gasped. Silence followed. "Lon Silver's? Jack?"

He lowered his voice. "I know, Bette. Hard. Yes. It's been months since you were there."

"Yes. Yes, months." She paused. "I was just thinking of him. My brother, I mean. So much on my mind lately. Since I was hurt, I wanted to see him. And since I got back he's been in my thoughts almost every day. Funny, when I'm working I can manage to go weeks without thinking of . . . what happened. Remembering that I have a little brother. But now? When I'm supposed to be resting? I've got too much time on my hands."

"I was hoping you would want to come," Jack replied.

"You must have picked up on something going on inside me. Yes. I do want to see him. Even at a distance. Okay. I'll come. Thanks, Jack."

"Great," Jack managed with a relieved sigh. "I have something to show Pastor Rankin in Jerusalem first, then I'll pick you up and then on to get Pastor Sykes."

"What a thrill," Bette returned.

23

The exterior door of the modest, second-floor office in East Jerusalem carried no company logo or name. Jack and Pastor Rankin shook hands with Walid Suliman, head of Palestinian Human Rights Watch.

"Thank you for seeing us," Jack said as they took their seats.

"It is my pleasure," the barrel-chested man with the short-cropped gray hair returned. "Even though you and I have not met before, Doctor Garrison, I understand you are a friend of Lev Seixas, whom I greatly admire. So tell me: how can I help?"

Jack gestured for Glen Rankin to take the lead in asking the questions.

"You are Palestinian?" Rankin asked.

"My mother," Suliman returned. "My father was Egyptian. The Muslim Brotherhood assassinated him and so we returned here from Cairo. I founded this organization in 1995."

"And you have no connection with Rights for Palestine?" Rankin inquired. "We . . . another pastor and I . . . met with Rafa Husseini of the RFP."

"Ah," Suliman returned. "No. She and I . . . let's just say that we see the path to peace in very different ways."

"But you are pro-Palestinian?" Rankin persisted.

Suliman spread his broad, fleshy palms. "I long for the day when a peaceful, prosperous Palestine lives in freedom alongside an equally peaceful and prosperous Israel."

"According to everything I have been taught," Rankin admitted, "Israel is the barrier to peace and prosperity. Is that not what you think also?"

"Do I like the restrictions on travel? No. Do I like border checkpoints and miles of fence? Not at all! But please consider this: the Israelis have no reason to want to be occupiers. It is terrorism that causes occupation, not the other way around."

"So how did we get to where we are today, and how do we fix it?"

Suliman raised an instructive finger. "In 1948 it is true that a half million Palestinian Arabs left the newly created Israel. The leaders of the Arab nations told them the move was only temporary; until Israel was destroyed. But when that was not accomplished, did any of those Arab nations welcome the refugees and offer to resettle them permanently? No!"

Suliman spoke with such vehemence that Jack was startled and Rankin blinked repeatedly.

The head of PHRW continued, "Did you know at that same time some seven hundred and fifty thousand Jews were expelled from Arab countries? From Morocco to Iran they came . . . and they were welcomed in Israel and made their lives over here. Yet do you ever hear of any Iraqi Jews demanding a right of return? Or a Libyan Jew wanting to reclaim family property confiscated in 1948? Of course not! The leaders of the Arab nations have used the Palestinian refugees for political, propaganda purposes for the last seventy years! And they still are!"

Suliman contemplated a framed, black-and-white photograph of a young couple posed very stiffly and dressed in the style of the early-sixties. Jack presumed it was a picture of Suliman's parents. After a long pause, Jack asked quietly, "Given that the Palestinian Authority and Hamas represent at least some local, self-government for the West Bank and Gaza, why doesn't life improve for the average Palestinian?"

Suliman muttered something under his breath before replying. "Abu Mazen . . . perhaps you know him as

Palestinian President Mahmood Abbas? He's worth about one hundred million dollars."

Rankin whistled.

Suliman nodded, then continued, "But his wealth is nothing compared to the earnings acquired by Khalid Mashaal, the head of Hamas. Mashaal is worth between two and three *billion* U.S. dollars . . . a lot actually acquired in U.S. dollars, I add, because of previous U.S. support, and U.S. money sent to UN missions for aid for Palestinian schools and hospitals and roads and factories. Billions of dollars!" Suliman pounded his fist on the desktop. "What hospitals? What factories?"

✡ ✡ ✡

Omar leaned against the wall across the street talking in a cell phone and gesturing with the cigarette in his other hand. "This is an opportunity," he hissed into the phone. "Suliman is long overdue for removal. I can take them both."

Rafa Husseini's voice in the receiver was insistent. *"Is the woman there? No. Is the old Jewish woman there? No. And you say there's an American Christian there? No, no!"*

"But the whole street is deserted, and I . . . "

"Enough! Too much risk and not enough gain. Follow them but do no more."

"As you say," Omar agreed. Punching the button he

savagely disconnected, then ground out the cigarette butt under his heel.

——————————— ✡ ✡ ✡ ———————————

"So you're saying corruption is a bigger cause of the suffering of the Palestinian people than Israel?" Rankin queried.

Suliman regarded him sadly. "Did you know that the UN has one department just for Palestinians . . . and another for all other refugees in the world? The United Nations has thirty thousand employees dedicated to helping with Palestinian issues. With so much help, why don't things get better? Because Abu Mazen knows that money from the West will stop flowing to a middle-class people with jobs. Have journalists ever shown Palestinians living in decent housing, some of them working in Israeli-owned factories? Never, because that is not the . . . what is the expression? That is not the script."

Jack and Pastor Rankin exchanged a look, but Suliman was not finished yet.

"The script . . . the script. You know when the narrative changed? From 1948 until the 1960s, it was the powerful Arab nations threatening poor, little Israel. But when the Palestine Liberation Organization was formed, they were very, very clever! They changed the story. Ever since then the script shows big, tough Israel bullying the poor Palestinians. Even the terminology changed."

"What do you mean?" Rankin asked. "Everyone knows about the Palestinians' wish for a homeland."

"When this land was governed by the British," Suliman corrected, "after the Turks in 1918, and up until 1948 . . . who were the Palestinians? The people who lived in the British Mandate of Palestine. The Jews lived in Palestine. They were Palestinians. Now, however, the whole world says there are no Jews who are Palestinians . . . just as there are no Palestinians who are treated fairly by Israel."

There was another lengthy pause in the conversation. At last Pastor Rankin offered, "My group . . . the denomination to which I belong . . . believes that economic pressure applied to Israel through Boycott-Divest-Sanction will aid the Palestinian cause. Don't you agree?"

Jack wondered what the response would be. No Israeli official . . . no Jewish citizen of Israel . . . could be pleased with an economic strangling of Israel. But what would be the reaction of a Palestinian? Even one who decried corruption in the Palestinian government might agree that the almighty dollar was the correct way to force additional concessions out of Israel.

"There are fifty thousand Palestinians working in Israeli-owned businesses and factories," Suliman responded. "Perhaps another fifty thousand who work without work permits, doing odd jobs and agricultural labor."

"But that's still only one percent of the Palestinian

population," Rankin objected.

Suliman shrugged. "True. But, with respect, why is it up to Israel to provide jobs for my people? Nor will you find support for BDS among my people who have jobs in Israel. Hey they earn twice as much working for an Israeli company as in the same job for a Palestinian firm . . . if there even were such jobs to be had. And every time a boycott or a sanction succeeds, and an Israeli factory closes . . . it's not just Jews who are hurt. Palestinians whose earnings supported their families lose their positions. When Israeli-owned SodaStream was pressured to shut its plant in the West Bank, five hundred Palestinians lost their jobs. BDS hurts my people . . . hurts the Palestinians.

"Do you remember what I said about longing for a peaceful Palestine alongside a peaceful Israel? That is at the heart of the matter. Until the Palestinians demand different leadership . . . honest leadership . . . that will change course and agree to coexistence with Israel . . . there will be no peace, and of course, no prosperity either."

There seemed very little left to say. Jack thanked Walid Suliman, then he and Pastor Rankin left the office.

☆ ☆ ☆

"That was . . . eye-opening, to say the least," Pastor Rankin commented as they exited from Walid Suliman's office.

"Someone who is Palestinian and committed to working for a free and stable Palestine . . . who doesn't blame Israel for the problems . . . and who thinks BDS does more harm than good."

"Would come as quite a shock to your PCUSA colleagues, I imagine," Jack observed.

Rankin waved his hands dismissively. "I was thinking more about college students. I have spoken on university campuses in Southern California. I've been in Political Science classes and Middle Eastern studies classes and even freshman current events seminars where the professor's every word dripped with hatred and scorn for Israel. I've recruited and encouraged students to march for BDS. I've seen Israeli flags ripped out of the hands of counter-protestors . . . flags that were then stomped on and burned."

Jack nodded. "You know, I have a lot to answer for as well," he admitted. "When I worked for the European Committee on Mid-East Policy, it was understood . . . a firmly held belief . . . that everything was Israel's fault. Except for a few open-minded members . . . who were quickly run off from the committee . . . ECMP did everything possible to injure Israel in business and diplomacy both."

"So what's next?"

"Back to pick up my grandmother, then Ms. Deekmann, and then Pastor Sykes. Then, I want you to see Ariel. A settlement in the 'Occupied West Bank.' But it may not be what you expect to find. Not at all."

✡ ✡ ✡

Neither Jack nor Glen Rankin paid any attention to the Arab man leaning against the wall, smoking the inevitable cigarette.

When they reentered their vehicle, Omar paused for two counts, and then tossed away the Marlboro before stabbing the buttons of the cell phone.

"Ariel," he reported. "The American, the old Baruch woman, and the young Jewish woman who killed your brother. All going to Ariel today."

Rafa Husseini's voice crackled in Omar's ear. *"Perfect! Pick me up."*

Omar disagreed. "I might lose them."

"Do you think I don't have other watchers around them?" Rafa insisted. *"Pick me up! I want to see their finish . . . or you don't get paid."*

24

On the drive along Route 5 to Ariel, Jack explained
where they were going and why . . . or at least, he tried to
explain. "It's a city located in the West Bank, and the site
of a university where Israelis and Arabs study together.
Jews, Arab-Israelis, Druze and Ethiopians all attend. It is a
showcase for what can happen when . . . "

Pastor Sykes snorted. "We know the *truth* about that
university. Built on land seized from the Palestinians.
Built to make Israeli occupation of Palestinian territory a
permanent reality. 'Showcase,' is right. We don't want to
hear from any handpicked puppets mouthing the words
the Israeli government tells them to say."

Dodi, seated between the pastors in the rear seat,

turned toward Glen Rankin. Rankin's face glowed bright red with what he now perceived as his colleague's rudeness. "The man we're going to meet is one of Ariel's founders," she said. "A dear man. Lon Silver. He's been the mayor and a member of the Knesset. And it's true that Ariel's location was selected to block an invading enemy from reaching Tel Aviv . . . but it's become much more than that. You'll see when we visit the university."

One thing no one mentioned was that on a previous visit to Ariel the car in which they had been riding had been shot at and Bette slightly wounded.

Today's arrival was uneventful.

Lon Silver was waiting for them on the plaza outside the engineering building. Silver had an unlit cigar clamped in his mouth, exactly the way Jack had last seen him.

"Shalom, shalom!" Silver boomed, clapping Jack on the back and pumping Rankin's hand vigorously. He saluted Bette and hugged Dodi.

Sykes ignored him, as if daring him to try to hug her, but Lon's greeting was cheerful enough to embrace them all. "Welcome! Come and meet my baby!"

Exiting the same building as the group entered, was a phalanx of college students. All were texting on their phones. All had backpacks slung over their shoulders, but the rest was all about variety. Three were male, two female. One of the women wore a Muslim hijab. One of the male students was bearded and wore a kippah. A second male student was tall, thin and black-skinned, and wore a white, pillbox shaped head covering.

Sykes stopped them just inside the entry doors. "Did you stage that just to demonstrate your diversity?" she demanded.

Silver, choosing to regard her comment as a joke, laughed. "Jewish-Israeli students. Arab-Israeli students. Palestinian students. Druze. Circassians. Jews from Ethiopia, and Jews from NYC! Go figure! They come here because our school," Silver patted a wall affectionately, "because our school is the most up-to-date in technology of anywhere in the world. Whole town has Wi-Fi. Rooms all have smart screens. We get lectures from professors in mathematics, robotics, high-tech agriculture . . . from all around the world. If it's high tech, then Ariel professors and students contributed to it: computer chips to drip-irrigation to cures for cancer. It's all happening right here."

Silver pushed open the door of a classroom. At the front of the room a half dozen students made notes on iPads while listening to a lecture from a television screen displaying a man in a white lab coat. At the back of the chamber two pairs of students fiddled with robots. One of their creations was vaguely humanoid but only a half meter tall. The other was equipped with fins and propellers for underwater propulsion.

"How do they do it?" Silver answered an unasked question. "I don't know. Geniuses! Not like me, eh? I'm an old shovel-and-hoe man myself."

Jack knew this self-deprecation was not really accurate but merely part of Silver's persona.

"So," Silver addressed Rankin and Sykes. "What other questions do you have before I take you out to see what you asked for?"

"You referred to Palestinian students. Is it difficult for them to gain admittance here?" Rankin offered politely.

Silver grunted and shifted the cigar to the other side of his mouth without using his hands. "Harder because of the paperwork," he admitted. "But not because we make it that way on purpose. They have to get travel permits, student visas, and they have to have security clearances. And the security checks hang some of them up . . . not because the student is a radical, but because maybe his uncle is in jail for arson."

Sykes snorted. Lon continued, "But there's no discrimination once a student enrolls here. Competition for graduate studies or research funding, yes! Racial or religious bigotry . . . who's got time for that? Shall we move on to the vineyard?"

✡ ✡ ✡

Dodi had disappeared somewhere with Lon's wife, Dorith.

Two small, potted grapevines and a shovel had been set out by Lon Silver for the visiting pastors to plant. It was an honor which Lon reserved for friends of Israel.

These American visitors were no friends of Israel.

Lon said quietly to Bette, "Officer Deekmann, there's not enough room in the golf cart for more passengers. I'll take the pastors on the tour of the vineyard. Why don't you and Jack sit awhile? There's a bottle of wine there on the table on the porch. Enjoy the afternoon. The grandkids will all be stopping by after school soon."

"All of them?" Bette's face fleetingly displayed emotion.

"Yes," he said kindly. "All."

The woman pastor interrupted, "These vines are all planted on Palestinian land, aren't they?"

Lon's smile faded and his complexion reddened as he took the wheel. He drew in his breath sharply and carefully considered his response. "There was nothing here for over two thousand years. Nothing. The land was barren before we came and planted . . . "

The woman remarked, "Barren or not, it was Palestinian none the less."

Lon explained, "No. It was territory of the Ottoman Turks for several centuries, and then after the Great War, the English took over governance. No Palestinians in sight."

She argued, "It's no wonder they want these vines pulled up . . . "

So the new grapevines and the shovel purposely remained behind as Lon drove the two off in the golf cart.

Jack knew the tour was an excuse for a hostile debate about why Israel had no right to exist.

Jack and Bette watched them drive toward the vineyard. Bette likewise seemed relieved to be out of range of the American's anti-Israel rants.

Lon's Australian shepherd jumped up from beneath a tree and trotted after his master. Dust from the retreating cart rose from the vineyard, creating the impression of Wiley Coyote chasing the Roadrunner.

Jack poured the chardonnay. Sun sparkled in the golden liquid.

"You're smiling?" Bette questioned.

Jack resisted the urge to comment on Wiley Coyote. Too American, he thought. Too random. "I was just thinking."

"Yes?"

"The wine." He held his glass up to the light. "Well, I mean, it's interesting that grapes have been grown here since . . ."

"Since always," Bette finished. "Yes." She inhaled the aroma. "And the vines nourished in soil where the patriarchs and prophets walked. My father used to talk about it. When he made the blessing over the wine for Shabbat. Yes. Papa would sip and close his eyes and say, 'So now we are tasting history.'"

Jack was relieved he had not mentioned what he had actually been smiling about. "That's beautiful. Really. I would have liked to have known your father."

Bette tucked her chin and looked away. "He would have liked you, I think."

"I wish . . ."

"Wishing can't change anything, Jack." She sipped the golden liquid. "Tasting history. My family helped plant these vines. Papa . . . his prayers are in the wine barrels and in the bottles and in this cup."

"Yet you have distanced yourself."

"To protect them!"

"But . . . your brother . . ."

"He doesn't know. And because the enemy of my family believes everyone in my house was killed, he is safe. Do you see, Jack? Benjamin must never know. That way he will never be known."

"What about you?"

"I know the face of Evil. And I am known. My grandfather, son of a great Sephardic Rabbi, gave testimony against the men who committed war crimes. Evil men were brought to justice. Their followers made an eternal vow against my grandfather's descendants. Didn't they tell you? Jack, it's something like, if you can picture it . . . in Lord of the Rings. I wear my family's history like the One Ring. I am the living memory of the Evil that came upon the Jews. Not just the Holocaust. Long before. It's a very ancient Evil. I'm still alive and the Dark Creature who hated my grandfather hates that fact. Evil knows my name, you see. I am proof of the promise God made to Abraham. I am still alive and still fighting. That is who we are. Children of Israel, you see. Now the eye of Sauron has turned toward me."

"You told me once; told me about your big family. You said . . . "

"Oh, that." She shrugged. "I just . . . I couldn't admit that it's just me and Benjamin. We are all who are left." Her voice trailed off.

The school bus lumbered up the road toward the turnoff. It stopped and Lon's grandchildren tumbled out. The afternoon sunlight gleamed on Benjamin's copper-colored hair. Bette's wistful gaze embraced the boy as he ambled toward the house with his siblings and cousins.

"He's a great looking kid," Jack observed. "My gosh, he looks so much like you."

Bette gave a little laugh. "Yes, he does. Except the red hair. My mother had red hair."

"And you look like her?"

A moment of longing crossed her face. "I have been told that."

"Then she was very beautiful."

"I took her family name after . . . after the massacre."

Benjamin in the midst of the other kids raised his hand and waved. The boy remarked, "Hey! It's Officer Deekmann and that American, Jack Garrison. We can practice our English," he informed the other kids.

"Shalom, children!" Bette called. "Your grandfather is giving a tour."

Benjamin laughed and swept his hand toward the vines. In almost perfect English he said, "Ah yes, the-Jews-making-the-desert-bloom-tour."

A girl of about nine chirped, "Where is grandmother?"

"Inside with *my* grandmother," Jack answered.

"And are you staying for supper?" Benjamin asked Jack.

Bette replied in Hebrew. "Not this evening, I'm afraid. The Americans we came with are not exactly the sort you want to spend an evening with."

Jack noticed how her eyes drank the boy in as the kids made their way up the steps and into the house. Their voices and laughter carried back to Jack and Bette. Someone turned on the television. Jack recognized the distinct *beep-beep* of a Road Runner cartoon.

He laughed. "Kids here watch that?"

"Of course. No dialogue. Just a metaphor for Israelis managing to outwit the Arab Coyote, eh?"

Jack agreed. "Of course."

Bette took another sip of Chardonnay. He's so happy," she said softly. "I know you understand. I only want him to be safe."

"Yes. I get it."

She searched his face. "Jack? It's why . . . same reason, you see? I feel the same about you."

Jack's smile was almost imperceptible. "Ironic."

"How so?"

"I mean that you deny yourself the freedom to love."

"It is because I love that I deny myself."

"Isn't that a victory for evil?"

"Benjamin is the last direct male descendant of the Chief Sephardic Rabbi. A lineage of thousands of years. My father used to say the devil has a long memory. If they knew . . . they would kill him. Like they murdered my family. And Jack, if they truly know who I am and knew I loved you, they would kill you, too. And one day, my children."

He was silent a moment. "Bette, every Jew can trace their line back to Abraham and Isaac and Jacob. Perhaps the names of our ancestors have been lost, but God knows who we are and where we come from. All of us were there when our fathers passed through the Red Sea. We . . . the children of Israel . . . are the living proof; we are witnesses that God's covenant is everlasting. That's why we are hated."

She nodded. "Yes. I know. But some ancient demon has made this personal. Personal against my grandfather, my father, my family, my brother. And against me."

"I won't let you go."

"You must. They told me in the hospital that my possible identity was suspected and mentioned in intercepted Hamas communications. I made up my mind. I won't have those I care for be collateral damage in an ancient war."

"Bette." He touched her hand. "I need you to look at me."

She looked away.

"Please don't, Jack. It's hard enough."

He sat back and swirled the wine in his glass. "The first public miracle of Jesus was at a wedding. Did you know that?"

"No."

"He turned water into wine. The best wine anyone had ever tasted. The master of the feast said he saved the best for last. Bette, I'm going to think about that. I will pray that, in your life, the best is being saved for last."

Kid's laughter rolled from the house as if music. Dust rose from the wheels of Lon's cart. The spell of truth was broken.

"Oh, look. They're back." Bette rose.

Jack followed her to meet them.

25

Leaving Jack's vehicle at the vineyard, Lon drove the guests in his roomier Land Rover. Jack was glad to be seated in the furthest back row beside Bette because Lon steered with one hand, while gesturing with his cigar and turning toward Pastor Rankin to reply to questions.

Thank goodness I'm keeping quiet and Rankin isn't seated clear back here, Jack thought.

Dodi and Pastor Sykes were in the middle row of seats.

Rankin and Silver chatted about the development of Ariel University into a first class educational institution and research facility, and then Rankin paused before continuing. "I already know how you're going to answer," Rankin suggested, "but I'd like . . . "

"So now you're a mind-reader?" Lon chided. "A good skill when someone is holding something back in confession, eh? But I might surprise you. Try me. Ask, already."

"I'd like to know if you think Israel is an apartheid state?"

Knitting his bushy eyebrows, Lon did not snap a hasty reply. "Try this on," he said. "In what countries in the Middle East is there freedom of worship . . . of conscience? Not in any Muslim countries." He fingered the gold Star of David necklace protruding from the unbuttoned top of his white shirt. "I couldn't wear this, could I? Would I even find a synagogue? And I don't just mean attacks on Jews either. Christians slaughtered in Egypt. Christians kidnapped in Nigeria. And that's not all, is it? ISIS destroying an ancient Christian monastery and an even older pagan Temple. And not just Islamic radicals, either. Go to Saudi Arabia as a non-Muslim and ask to visit Mecca? Sheesh! Freedom of worship in Iran? Ha! Death for trying to convert a Muslim. Death for a Muslim if he converts. Death for 'insulting the Prophet.' So you tell me: if apartheid means treating minorities like second-class citizens under a load of restrictions, where is there more evidence of that? Israel, or everywhere else in the region?"

Jack looked out the window. They had been driving through vineyards from the moment the route swept them outside of Ariel. Like the two-lane road, the orderly vines spiraled around a hillside. At the top Lon wheeled the

Land Rover into a parking lot carrying a sign in Hebrew. Underneath it repeated the name in English: *Rechelim Winery*.

"We're here already?" Jack said.

"I think this is what you asked for, Jack. But take a minute and enjoy the view."

Jack, Bette, and Glen Rankin readily complied. From atop the conical hill, vineyards sprawled in every direction, parting in the near distance to embrace a small village. A southerly breeze swirled past the hilltop, carrying with it the aroma of . . . what? Jack pondered. *Smells like lighter fluid.*

No one noticed the weather-beaten Mercedes that pulled into the parking area one row of vehicles away, nor gave a glance to the woman who drove, or the man in the passenger seat.

"Just under nine hundred meters above the sea," Lon continued. "Snow sometimes in winter! One hundred eighty acres of vines. Cabernet, Shiraz, Merlot, Viognier . . . lots more. You remember helping me plant vines, yes?" he asked Jack.

Jack nodded, recalling the extraordinary feel; the unexpected connection he experienced. On that visit, Jack had not even known of his own Jewish heritage, but somehow handling the earth of the Jewish homeland had made his senses tingle. "Of course."

"Well, this," Lon swept his cigar around the hillside. "This is what I want my baby vines to grow up to be! Lots of memories here, too," he added. "Rechelim . . . plural of Rachel. So: The Rachels. With his cigar Lon touched each of three stubby fingers in turn. "Rachel the Matriarch, of course. But also Rachel Drouk, who was killed near here in an ambush on a bus. I knew her. Also to honor another Rachel; Rachel Weiss who was murdered in a bus bombing near Jericho. After Rachel Drouk was killed, women and children moved here from all over Samaria. Lived in tents. Said this was home. Crazy people, us Jews, eh? Defied the government and the Palestinians to move them. So: here they stayed."

Pastor Sykes and Dodi joined the group. "Stolen land," Sykes repeated.

Lon shrugged. "You'll not find many Palestinians here who object."

"What do you mean, 'here?'" Sykes demanded.

"There are eighty Palestinian employees who work just at this winery alone, who get their paychecks here, get other benefits here," Lon said quietly. "Would you like to meet some of them?"

Before Rankin could agree or Sykes say "No," the tour was interrupted.

On the rising wind a half-dozen objects soared into view. Like ill-omened birds, the objects flapped in the breeze as they floated toward the hilltop. They also trailed dark gray fumes.

"Missiles?" Jack said in response to Bette's pointing. As

the group watched, black eggs dropped from the sky-born attack, bursting into flame before hitting the ground.

"Incendiary kites," Lon corrected. "They're aiming at the winery. Bette, drive your grandmother and our guests back to my place. Jack, will you stay? The firefighters may need help."

"I want to help too," Rankin offered.

————————————————   ✩ ✩ ✩   ————————————————

"A perfect distraction," Omar noted from the passenger seat of the Mercedes. He pushed the door ajar. "Let me get out now. They are all watching the sky. They'll never know what hit them."

"I agree," Rafa Husseini challenged. "But who needs you? They are all together! I can do this myself!"

Revving the Mercedes' engine to a screaming pitch, she yanked it into gear and the vehicle leapt forward. Omar, half in and half out of the car, was spun around, and then dragged forward as his shirtsleeve caught on the doorframe.

————————————————   ✩ ✩ ✩   ————————————————

Jack was the first to notice the vehicle attack. At that moment he saw it all as if in slow motion . . . and also a replay of what he had experienced before: he saw again

the Israeli policewoman knifed in Jerusalem . . . he saw
the tumbling, broken bodies after the assault on London's
Westminster Bridge . . . he saw Bette's crumpled and
broken form after she saved his life in Hebron by taking the
assassin's knife herself.

"Not this time!" he shouted.

Shoving Bette one direction and Dodi the other, Jack
drew the Jericho pistol from the waistband of his trousers.
Coolly, he squeezed off shots that hit the windshield of the
Mercedes, blasting it into a thousand fragments.

At that moment, one of the fire-kites dropped its
flaming cargo directly onto the car's roof, rolling down to
the missing windshield, and into the driver's seat.

There was a shriek of mingled pain and terror and a
sudden jerk of the steering wheel that deflected the car's
path . . . causing it to collide with Pastor Sykes, who was
knocked to the ground.

In the next moment, the man being dragged along
beside the car freed himself. He rolled over twice, but came
up running away, apparently uninjured.

The Mercedes reached the edge of the parking area,
bumped against the low concrete slab that defined the limit
of the asphalt, and plunged over it toward the brink of the
hill.

Teetering there a moment while screams from the
interior continued, it launched over the edge of the
cliff-face, rolled end-over-end before reaching the bottom,

where it lay upside down, engulfed in thick, black smoke.

✧ ✧ ✧

"Are you alright?" Jack asked Dodi.

"Of course, dear," his grandmother agreed. "I'm a tough old bird."

Bette knelt beside the prone figure of Pastor Sykes. "Don't move," Bette instructed. "*Mogen David Adom* is already on the way. We'll get you to hospital right away."

Through bloody lips and broken teeth, Sykes muttered. "Never would have happened if the Palestinians had their own land. This is Israel's fault. All of it."

"Come on, Jack," Lon said. "And you, Pastor Rankin, if you want. One of those kites landed on a stack of oak barrels. We need to keep the fire from spreading to the buildings."

Jack looked back at Bette. "*Go on,*" she mouthed. "*I'm okay.*" And then, "*I love you.*"

EPILOGUE

Bette had stammered through her phone conversation with Lon Silver.

Jack heard the big man laugh when she asked the question.

"Of course, Bette! It's about time the boy knows he has a sister who happens to be one of Israel's Wonder Women."

"When?" Bette breathed urgently. "When can I come?"

"This afternoon." Lon replied. "Bring Jack if you like. We'll make sure Benjamin is there." He hesitated a moment. "Bette, he knows a few details. That he came to our family when he was a tiny baby after a tragedy. He believes he is the only . . . "

"I should have told him. No one should be the only one."

And so it was agreed. Bette and Jack set out in silence.

The world was waking up from the long winter's sleep.

Beyond the cultivated fields of Ariel, wild flowers bloomed like a patchwork quilt.

A cloud of dust followed the car up the curve of the vineyard road. Bette's heart raced a little faster as sunlight glinted on the windows of Lon Silver's house.

Jack glanced toward Bette. "You okay?"

"No."

"It'll be good. Lon is a wise man."

"Just a little nervous." Bette gazed at the new buds on the vines.

"New beginnings are never easy." Jack placed his hand over hers.

She raised his fingers to her lips and kissed them. "Thank you, Jack. Thank you. I want to begin again. With all my heart."

"I love you, Bette."

The yard in front of the house was empty. Jack parked. Bette unfastened her seat belt and stepped out into the afternoon light.

The aroma of baking bread wafted from the house. Bette closed her eyes.

She remembered her mother in the kitchen, kneading bread for Shabbat. Mama smiled over her shoulder at

Bette and said, "Bette, would you please take care of the baby while I finish?"

It was as though no years had passed since Mama made the request.

Take care of the baby? The baby had grown into a handsome, bright boy.

Bette answered her mother once again, "Yes, Mama."

The memory was beautiful and clear. The screen door of the Silver house opened and young Benjamin, awkward and eager, stepped onto the porch. He had Mama's red hair and the crooked smile of Papa. His eyes were the color of Bette's eyes.

Unmistakable. Her brother.

Benjamin tucked his chin slightly and raised his hand in greeting. "Shalom . . . Bette," he said shyly. "I was hoping you would come."

"Oh, Benjamin!" Bette opened her arms wide and moved toward him. "I'm here. I'm here!"

The boy cried out. Reaching for her, he stumbled down the steps and fell into his sister's embrace.

AN OPEN INVITATION

If you would like take the step that will connect you with Yeshua . . . . Jesus the Messiah . . . consider this:

Jesus came from heaven to show us "the Way, the Truth and the Life." (John 14:6) He died on the cross for our sins and rose from the dead on the third day. He says, "Behold, I stand at the door and knock, and if any man hears my voice, and opens the door, I will come in to him, and sup with him, and he with me." (Rev. 3:20)

You can have a personal relationship with God through Jesus Christ. In a simple prayer, tell Him you know you are a sinner, and ask forgiveness. Tell Him you believe He died for your sins, rose from the dead, and you want to invite Him to come into your heart. Tell Him you want to follow Him as your personal Lord and Savior, in His Name.

And if you would like more information on how to grow spiritually, please visit www.raybentley.com

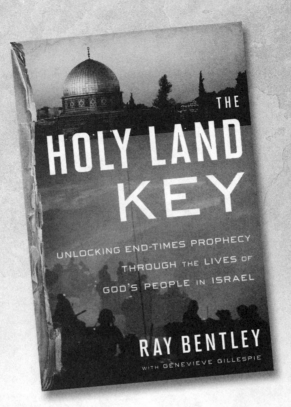

For more books by Bodie Thoene, visit:
WWW.THOENEBOOKS.COM

START FROM THE BEGINNING WITH JACK GARRISON....

"*On the Mountain of the Lord* is a thriller, superimposed over Biblical prophecy, history, and geography ... I'm already looking forward to their next novel."

—Anne Graham Lotz

Order book one today at
RAYBENTLEY.COM